'Beautiful writing and a modest, pensive protagonist contrast grisly violence as we follow a stalker through a maze of streets and shops in Benedictus's *Consent*. Intrigued by those more colourful than he, drawn to the vibrant and vivacious, the narrator is trapped in his irrelevance and we inside his head as he records the movements and the moments of his more ostentatious prey. A brilliant and goosebumpy read!' Susan Crawford

'Part crime, part thriller, part horror novel from the much-praised author of *The Afterparty* . . . This is a disturbing book that makes the reader complicit in the narrator's voyeurism.' *Tatler*

'An almighty page-turner that will have you in its grip until the final page.' *Bookmunch*

'A fascinating, disturbing and original thriller that erases the boundaries of the genre and draws challenging new ones.' Sophie Hannah

Leo Bene[illegible]tus is a freelance feature [illegible] *Gu[illegible]* and other publicatio[illegible] [illegible] *Afterparty*, was published in 2011 by Jonathan Cape.

www.leobenedictus.co.uk

Further praise for *Consent*:

'*Consent* has a claustrophobic intensity that makes it a memorable and rewarding experience.' *Sunday Express*

'What is perhaps most unsettling is the narrator's voice: philosophical and apparently possessing self-knowledge (he is well versed in Montaigne), yet deeply deranged . . . There is no denying the ingenuity with which Benedictus constructs his tale . . . [he] ensures that the familiar elements are outweighed by his innovative approach.' *Financial Times*

'The queasy set-up offers an undeniable frisson of black comedy, partly because the narrator is so implacably deadpan in the face of his wildly escalating misdeeds . . . But what's funniest and most biting is the book's unexpected satire of gender relations . . . *Consent* is thought-provoking as well as shocking, with a teasing parallel between stalking and the business of fiction writing itself. It's a high-wire act for sure, but one that doesn't trivialise the issue at the novel's obsidian heart.' *Metro*

'Mean and darkly addictive, it provides neither the twists nor the resolutions of a conventional thriller and is somehow all the more unsettling for it.' Hephzibah Anderson, *Mail on Sunday*

'Like Benedictus's excellent debut, *The Afterparty*, this is a novel that plays with the conventions of the form, asking the reader to consider his or her place in the forming of the narrative. With great subtlety and wit, Benedictus shows us how close our own relentless curiosity about the lives of the characters in the book is to the deranged obsessions of the narrator. The unexamined compacts that form between author and reader are held up for inspection, and we see new and unsettling strangeness in the everyday. It all makes for an unusual and enormously compelling novel.' Alex Preston, *Observer*

'Such a great read and the product of a highly entertaining and disturbingly dark mind.' Stephen Mangan

'A fiendishly clever book, though not for the soft-hearted . . . You'll find yourself turning pages in the most disturbing kind of grip.' *Sydney Morning Herald*

'In his new work, another clever, cutting riff on the book-within-a-book (and possibly another book) trope, Benedictus keeps himself off the pages – thankfully so, as the anonymous protagonist speedily evolves from routine sociopath to extreme psychopath.' Catherine Taylor, *Guardian*

CONSENT

LEO BENEDICTUS

First published in the UK in 2018
by Faber & Faber Limited
Bloomsbury House, 74–77 Great Russell Street
London WC1B 3DA
This paperback edition first published in 2019

Typeset by Faber & Faber Ltd
Printed and bound by CPI Group (UK) Ltd, Croydon, CR0 4YY

A CIP record for this book
is available from the British Library

ISBN 978–0–571–33590–9

2 4 6 8 10 9 7 5 3 1

CONSENT

I DO NOT CONSIDER MYSELF a complicated person. I don't think many people are. I accept that I have lived strangely for the past four years, and for the past month especially, so I suppose I must consider myself strange, but please forgive me if I don't wear the word with the best grace. I am not so strange that I take pride in it. I have only tried to live by simple principles with doggedness and honesty, and with an open mind.

Now and then I believe we all glimpse the simplicity of ourselves, whether or not we try. For instance I'm sure you've heard people who've nearly died saying that *it reminds you what's important,* by which they mean that the list of things is shorter than they thought. Soon enough most return to worrying about bills and popularity and lateness. In order to forget life, they get on with living. Those who stay reminded are considered traumatised.

Danger forces this grim wisdom on you, but it is by no means the only route. Most children discover at some point that minds can be boiled down pretty easily by playing a game of *Why?* Just ask *Why?* of any statement, then ask

Why? of the answer, and continue to ask *Why?* until you get stuck in a loop, or you reach particle physics, or the grown-up gets bored, whichever is the soonest.

Let me give you an example. *Why?* Because examples are a good way to explain things, and right now I'd rather explain this idea than get on with the story. *Why?* Because I'm anxious. *Why?* Various reasons. Among them, because I'm making tea in the dark. *Why am I making tea in the dark?* Good question. Because I want to bring her something comforting when I go upstairs, but I don't dare turn on the lights. *Why don't I dare?* Because I don't want to risk waking her. *Why?* Because I want to wake her later, at the right time. *Why?* Because I want to make a good impression. *Why do I want to make a good impression?* Because I want to be loved. *Why do I want to be loved?* I don't know. Curiosity I suppose. I want to find out what it's like. *Why do I want to find out?* I don't know.

Actually it is not completely dark in here, if I'm going to be accurate, which I plan to be. The kettle's power indicator light gives an orange glow to the waiting cups. The point is it's dark enough to be anxious about tea-making, on top of all the other things.

We are in the hissing stage. You know the hissing stage? The kettle begins silently, then there are clicks, then the clicks give way to a quiet hissing that becomes loud. That's where we are, in the becoming.

Her cup is white with a blue feather pattern painted on it. She has an especial fondness for the blue feather design. I don't know why. I only know that whenever one is available, that's what she chooses, and this must be a matter of policy because she has a varied, even a raucous, cup shelf. There is another feather cup, but I've chosen something different for myself because I worry that if I choose the same it will look like I am trying to be neat instead of thoughtful. And I can't just say to her, *Oh, by the way, I've given you one of your favourite cups.* That's not subtle. That sounds like bait for praise. I'll just let her notice that my cup is different, an obscure green and gold one from the back of the shelf that she rarely uses. Hopefully she'll understand that I intend it as a modest contrast, like the white of a gallery wall or of the page. It may not work, but I believe in doing more than is required. You can't control what people think, but if you do everything you can, they'll notice, and understand that the great trouble you've taken must mean you care. You must show almost a mild madness.

I am also anxious, as I say, and looking for distractions. I know it is ridiculous to believe that the glow of the kitchen lights might find a way to penetrate her bedroom door upstairs, but I managed it, and left the room dark. My roving torch beam I worried would draw attention to the windows, so I switched it off. I'm left with this orange gloom, which gives a rather forbidding atmosphere. That and the weather. It is a windy night out there. When the gusts come they sound determined to scare me. I shiver sometimes.

Now we're at the rumbling stage. I lift the kettle. I don't wait for it to boil. Perhaps you've noticed before that kettles often spend a long time on the threshold of a hundred degrees, turning water into steam. It's pointless, when ninety-five degrees would do just as well. I'm also anxious about the noise. Lifting the kettle disconnects the power and switches off the orange light. I forgot that and it alarms me, being in complete darkness with almost boiling water. I manage to put the kettle back on the counter but I still can't see anything. At last I find the handle of the fridge and open it, bathing everything in whiteness. I should have done this before. I aim the water at the dark regions of the teabag. I get milk out of the fridge and fetch a spoon. She likes her tea strong and unsweetened, the milk stopped at chestnut, but this is difficult to judge in low light, so I carry her cup closer to the fridge. Clouds of vapour fill the shelves, but I am satisfied. I take the teabag out and drop it in the bin, which smells of onions, remembering to open and close the lid as quietly as I can. They clang like bells, the lids of pedal bins. My tea I make the same.

The rest of my stuff is in a sports bag which I strap to my shoulders, gripping the torch in my mouth, while carrying both cups of tea. Bags of this kind are not designed for shoulders, and my socks are slippery on the floor, so I cross the hall and take the stairs with caution. I go stealthily, scanning each step. I nudge through her door.

She sleeps. Keeping the torch beam off her face, I place the feathered cup on the bedside table, and my own beside my bag on the carpet. I take her phone and unplug the wire, being careful neither to jolt the tea nor dislodge her open book and lose the page.

She lies on her side. Her face is half-hidden by her hair, which is heavy and lustrous. As I watch, her sleeping finger hooks it back behind an ear. She chews the air and exhales, settling. I wonder what she's dreaming about. Perhaps it's dreams of her girlhood, of growing up fatherless but in secure circumstances in a small town. Or of spending her young years well enough liked at school and known for brains, mostly a historian, then shaking the reputation off at university. After university I know that she was sharper with herself and found a well-paid job, and it turned out that money suited her. From her stalky adolescence, glamour came. Even so she was very surprised at first by all the men who propositioned her. This was in that tender stage of first employment when, you understand, still wary in the world, she presumed with sadness that being pestered for sex was just the burden that a woman carried until she carried children. Plus she presumed that these were not prime men. Over time, however, and by gathering the remarks of friends, she came to know that she was beautiful. It can't just be shrugged away, all that beholding, though it gave her the haughty tilt that she had feared. There began to be a distance in her voice. She served rejections briskly. When the job became yet better paid she bought this little house. Friends said it was unlike her to be so spontaneous in a matter of weight, but looking back they agree that there were always glints of firmness. Until recently she was known at work for steady hands. Now they clutch around under the covers. I watch her eyelids wriggling. Her breaths go shallow and disordered. I look at her and I think, You can't see me, but I am here.

She dreams.

FIRST I SHOULD EXPLAIN how I got rich.

It happened quite suddenly four years ago, on the day of my aunt Kathy's funeral. Those few of us present met afterwards to exchange memories in a smart restaurant closed for the occasion. They were dull memories, but it was a Friday afternoon so we drank freely. We needed to. The place was far too big. There was plainly a wine surplus, and a long table stood against a wall stacked handsomely with sandwiches, pastries and prepared fruit. People like to say there is an unmentionable elephant in the room at such times, but we actually had space for one and could have fed it.

Myself, I was very hungry and ate all I could. I took something from a different serving plate each time, hoping to leave them tousled as if by a crowd. Others nibbled too, and in the end we left what could easily have been the aftermath of thirty or forty mourners with small appetites, which you might expect given the occasion and the time of day. Besides, whoever cleared up afterwards would have to be quite paranoid to imagine someone systematically visiting different plates in order to deceive them.

Kathy's lawyer made his approach while I was eating

strawberries, I think. Having established who I was, he gave me his card, said he had some documents that concerned me and suggested we meet afterwards to discuss it. I admit I expected something gestural from Kathy. I also admit that I knew that a gesture from her would not be very small. She'd been single and a heavy earner, one of the first women to make a mark in banking, though the career was no crusade. She was as uninterested in the women's movement as she was in everybody else's. You only had to be with her twenty minutes to see the stern fixity of a person who expects nothing from their fellows and gives less back. She must have been an anvil to haggle with. It's mostly visual now, my memory of Kathy. It's the bright suits and glasses, and the fringe that changed colour but never shape. The cancer news she took not happily, of course, but nevertheless in a spirit that was close to vindication, death in your fifties being a Pyrrhic victory over the optimists, you might say. Any talk of battling during a visit and you'd be dismissed. I just liked to ask how it felt, knowing she would die soon, and I think she liked my bluntness. On good days she said she was glad not having to worry about the grief of others. On bad ones she said almost nothing.

I don't want you to think that Kathy didn't laugh, however. That last stage saw a flourishing of bitter humour. A couple of times a joke seemed on the point of finishing her off. The best way to go, I suppose, if you can manage it. In particular she developed a running theme about her *legacy*, as though she were an outgoing chief executive or politician, which made me laugh as well. I thought it indicated that she knew she'd been a pioneer. Later I wondered whether the joke had another layer she'd been keeping to herself, because Kathy left a legacy indeed.

Having been solemn before, the lawyer gave me a lot of grins in the taxi. We made no smalltalk. At his office he ordered coffee and while I drank mine explained that, after a donation to the hospice and a few sideways odds and ends, it was my aunt's wish that all her wealth should go to me. Once you combined the various accounts and funds with a conservative valuation of her flat, this amounted to just less than eleven million, a sum that has only grown in the years since. I find even the interest difficult to spend.

At the time my main feeling was confusion over how to react.

So I'm rich? I said, or something like it.

The lawyer agreed.

How do people normally react?

This question seemed to surprise the lawyer. He said it was hard to generalise, because cases this dramatic were rare. Indeed when you considered the amount of money involved and the unexpectedness, this was among the most dramatic he had handled in more than thirty years. He did not know what you'd call normal.

But you are smiling, I said. And it seemed you were looking forward to telling me, so you must have expected something good. Did you expect me to be pleased?

He said most people were pleased.

What do they do?

They didn't exactly celebrate, at least not in his office, but he could see they were excited. Some had problems that would be solved by the bequest, and they often cried. Some cried at feeling so beloved by the deceased. A few times he'd had to convince people he was really a lawyer. It varied.

That night I gave my aunt's memory a maudlin evening with a bottle of whisky. Saturday I went a little crazy on the town. Restored and ready for work on Monday, I stopped at my breakfast bowl. We'll say that the spoon was halfway to my lips, although of course I can't remember. The radio was definitely on, some squabble about trains. It had been my plan to bide time and let the circumstances sit with me before making any big decisions, yet there was something absurd now about having breakfast just as I always did, my glum life unchanged even by this shock. I had a job that I neither loved nor hated. Why would I give my day to that? It's hard to explain but it was like I'd stepped off stage to join an audience watching my own acting. *Eats breakfast with the radio on. Does nothing hasty.* All weekend I'd believed myself set free by Kathy's money, but that was quite wrong. I'd been free all my life and refusing to know it. If you don't look closely, biding time and killing it look about the same.

Free then, and rich enough to do anything, what should I do? This was what I had to think about, and it was almost a curse. It was a curse. I got quite upset. I can't remember making a decision about work or informing my colleagues that I wasn't coming in. I think there were some emails later in the week. What I remember is going out. Emotionally I was a shaken keg and I hoped that being outside would put in embarrassment as a stopper. I also had a question I couldn't answer and I've often noticed – I don't know if you're the same? – that I do my best thinking in the margins, when

I'm half-doing something else. Anyway, very distressed, in desperation really, I went for a walk because it was either that or freaking out at home.

It was early, and there were still commuters. The current went towards the city centre, so I went the other way. A bus pulled up beside me, so I got on, and stayed on to the depot. I took another, and when that terminated, another. Looking through the windows made me calmer. Calmer but not calm. Like I was shuffling myself, that's the best way I can describe it. I had a need to behave strangely.

Perhaps as a result I remember feeling terribly conspicuous. I expected to be challenged by one of the other passengers and asked what I was up to, in answer to which I would have wet myself or begun to scream or throw up, and disembarked when the next stop came. However, in time peculiarity became me. I stopped worrying and started seeing things. A middle-aged foreign couple. They had new luggage and were in the advanced stages of getting lost. Where they wanted to be, this far from any sights or big hotels, had me beat too. The man held a page from a notebook and he and his wife (as I presumed) would point to bits of it now and then and there'd be light bickering. Treated reverently at first, the page was increasingly often slapped and snatched around, and in the end became a kind of baton for making accusations. You could see it had mostly been his plan because she did most of the accusing. They were bourgeois, judging by the luggage, which I think was an ingredient in things, public transport being a nuisance that at home they were proudly unfamiliar with. (But taxis here being too expensive.) Other passengers tried to provide help but were soon rebuffed by all the nodding. When in the end they got off it was not triumphantly, not laughing, their destination spied, but grim with the acceptance that they'd come too far. As we pulled away I watched them face each other on the pavement, taking turns to be angry. I got off myself at the next stop and ate lunch.

After lunch I saw Laura D, who was my first. She took a double seat three rows ahead of me and gave one to her bag. She was on the phone, so I heard her too. I'm sure we all did. Perhaps you've never noticed how the prettier girls on trains and buses talk more loudly than the others? And they make a proper racket laughing.

Laura was a hairdresser, but queenly in her ways and limbed like a Matisse. She was telling a friend about the foibles of an old woman client, while journeying to the woman's home. The great size and peculiar furnishings of the place were mentioned, as was the otiose use of her name all the time, like *Laura* was a maid or something. Worst was the client's intransigence, now never questioned, over the order in which the different sections of her hair had to be cut and coloured. Laura doubted whether the distinguished husband, always absent, was even real. Others I am sure looked sourly on this exposure of the old woman she was about to go and serve so falsely. People don't like that kind of thing because it makes them look for the false servants in their own lives. I was taken with it however, because something did not ring true. I'd like to be able to say what exactly. Maybe Laura spoke too fluently, or forcefully, but she seemed to want to be overheard. Also her bag seemed small for all the equipment she said she was carrying. Shortly before standing for her stop she sprayed herself from a bottle of perfume. Would she do that before this bothersome old lady? All I can say now is that I quickly developed a kind of belief that there was some secret here, and a need to know if the belief was right. When she got off, I got off with her. That was the beginning.

—

Was it the beginning? I'm having to write this in snatched moments here and there, which is not convenient. Things generally are difficult right now for reasons that I'll come to. But the spells between are a chance to think freshly. And I don't know. I look back and I don't know when all this started. The thing with Laura, Kathy's death, the thing now, me writing, me growing up, when you put them in a line they make a kind of sense. More sense than at the time. Did I really find my new life on the first day of looking? Much easier to believe it was already somewhere in me. This is what people call hindsight I suppose. First it's hard to explain things, then it's hard not to generate explanations.

Then it's different. At other times it feels like everything happened to someone else, what's happened recently especially.

I'm sorry. I'm not explaining myself well. Have I been someone all my life who would do what I've done? Or am I just somebody who did? I suppose that's what I'm asking.

Because I've thought a lot about how I'll look when your eyes leave these pages for the final time, perhaps before the final page. I wonder if you'll see a monster, and if I am one, or if monstrosity is a costume to be tried on.

Why am I so nervous? I am new to storytelling, it is true. A greenhorn at the inkhorn you might say, but I've been ready for nerves and am quite pleased with the start I've made, though I do do a lot of doubting. I get so wrapped up in the events I'm making an account of that when I pause to look again it's like the music stops, the lights go on, and I'm surrounded by droops of bunting and lost coats and forgotten inches of wine. I get self-conscious suddenly. I've undone dozens of beginnings. Who knows if even this paragraph will stand? Probably that's how it always is. Probably all beginnings begin with grief for the lost conviction of intending.

You're being very patient. You want the nitty-gritty, and you're right. Laura: what went on there? Me: who am I? A complicated question about anyone, I'm sure we can agree. Well I am a rich man, as you have heard, and neither young nor old. You know my name. My occupation is not so easy. The word that many would apply to me is *stalker*, but applying doesn't make it so. I'd say instead that I practise people studies. Studying people is what I do so if it needs one that can be its name.

Be assured that I'm not hiding from the facts of things. I do secretly follow strangers on the street. I wait outside their houses and I listen to their conversations, if I can. Look through my notes, which fill a cabinet, and you will find some men named, but on the whole I study women. Which women? I don't think I can generalise. A subject need only interest me for a moment, as Laura did, and I am on them. When someone more interesting comes along, I switch to them. It's rare for me to study anybody longer than a month. Most I'm finished with inside a week or so.

Nevertheless you'll think – and this is obviously a paraphrase, I don't presume to know your thoughts exactly – that following women around the way I do is an invasion of their privacy, perhaps worse. That's partly why I'm telling you about it now, having never told anyone before, so I can show that I expect no more privacy for myself than I grant others. My subjects do not choose to be my subjects, it is true, but only because such a choice is impossible. If you volunteer to be studied, you stop being you.

Try it yourself. That's another thing I'm saying. Go out, pick somebody and watch them. Take your phone and a notebook. Persist. You've probably already tried, mildly. What begins as a confluence of yours and another person's journeys, on the train maybe or leaving a cinema, gets into an entanglement. Maybe you both sense it. Maybe just you do. You follow, feeling that it's not really following because you're going the same way, then when they at last reach their office you feel the clutch of a goodbye. It's normal. How many times do you think the person being followed has been you?

—

Laura crossed the road. I went with her. She turned into a long avenue lined with characterful brick merchant houses and linden trees. I turned too. I let the space between us lengthen. Soon she was just a dark rhythm and a swinging bag. Then she wasn't there. Instantly I regretted my coolness and sped up, then ran. I reached a cobbled mews, a beautiful old pub at the end of it. A pub and a few garages and flats. Nothing resembling a grand old lady's mansion in anyone's eyes. I stopped to catch my breath, leaning against a panel of doorbells as if about to ring one. Laura took a seat in the pub, by the window. Relief. Joy and relief. The cold brim of a shiver swept across me.

As best I could, I squared things. There was a chance that Laura had received word of a postponement or a cancellation after I'd lost sight of her, and had gone into the pub to wait. Only a small chance though. Seeing her bustle along, it also seemed unlikely she was early. Meeting in the pub might of course be one of the client's eccentricities, but Laura had not mentioned it on the phone, and she'd seemed set on mentioning everything.

If at first I had been curious, now I was obsessed. I had to move away from the doorbells when an elderly man walked out and gave me a look. This left just the street to wait on. It was odd to loiter outside on a cold day, though I was glad of the excuse to keep my face in my lapels. (Now I always carry cigarettes, which make immaculate pretexts for hanging around on the street. You can also bury yourself in your phone, or pretend to be talking on it, but this calls for more boldness than I had at the time, and can be distracting.)

Presently, a man came to sit with Laura. A well-dressed

man, expected by her, but older than I'd guessed. She had white wine. He chose mineral water, and got the conversation going. She said little, but was flirting, you could see. It was in her long stares and in the scale of her laughing. Flirting meant that they were not already lovers. On the table she had a pen and notebook, which she was hardly using. She wanted something from him but he wasn't giving it, or not giving all of it, that's what I inferred. I've noticed since that you can sometimes see people more plainly without speech to misdirect you. The man stood up, shook Laura's hand, said *Good luck*, I think, and left. They'd been together for ten minutes at most.

What had I witnessed? The lying to her friend, the notebook and her flirtatious ways made clear that the occasion was important to Laura, but less to him. He seemed like someone powerful, though light with it, and gracious in the obdurate art of being petitioned. I can't say why, but to me he also appeared decent. Like someone she should trust. Ducking behind a van, I watched her leave soon afterwards. I felt I had no choice but to follow her home.

I've been doing a lot of physical work recently, more than I'm used to, and I seem to have wrenched something in my shoulder. There was no one incident, or not one that I noticed. When I woke up a couple of days ago it just went stiff, and since then has been given to spasms. It's not terrible. I only feel it if I reach for something at the wrong angle, or lift much weight. Then a belt of pain flashes down my neck. The rest of the time I feel nothing. Like at the moment, typing is fine.

The odd thing though, the reason I bring this up, is that I find I can't help looking for the pain. I wave my arm around trying to find the exact bad angle, or probe the muscles with my left hand. When I succeed it hurts, so I stop. Then I drift into the search again. Versions of this self-torture are quite common, I believe. I've often been like this over pulled muscles or mouth ulcers, flicking the pain on and off like you might play with a hair clip. But only with certain kinds of pain. I'd never aggravate a cut on my finger, or a burn. Once I broke a rib. Have you ever broken a rib? In most cases there's no treatment. The intercostal muscles hold the bones in place and eventually they set. After the first few days they smoothly rise and fall with normal breathing and you don't feel anything. Then you laugh. Or worse you sneeze, and the pain is terrible. Terrible. When I had that broken rib and I felt a sneeze coming I'd start trying to sneeze, hoping to trick it into fading away, as sneezes like to do.

What is it about some pains that makes you fidget with them, even while you avoid others? It's to do with hiddenness, I think. I'm anxious about this shoulder because I don't know quite where the pain is, so I could make the wrong move and it might strike. It's like the threat of being afflicted is worse than the affliction. The threat starts to rule you, which changes what you think about who you are. Personally I'd rather be the cause of my own pain than live as it dictates.

I worried horribly about being seen by Laura on her journey back across the city, and between times I worried horribly about losing her again. All I needed to do was keep a calm distance, as I know now, but instead like some capering cartoon I lurked and peeped and fiddled with my shoelaces the whole way to her house. Too large a house to be hers alone, it seemed to me, and too suburban and well tended for a rental between friends. It was her parents', you had to guess, the scene of a childhood outgrown, or overdue to be. No way was it Laura in the front garden deadheading the narcissi. I felt I'd known her long enough to be sure of that.

From here the thing was easy, but not quick. The next morning I returned and waited outside a postal depot checking my phone. It was the nearest plausible place to stand but not too near. I had to stare hard to be sure I wouldn't miss her leaving. But I did miss her leaving, I can only suppose, because at ten o'clock I decided I could wait no longer and gave up.

That's one of the times this could have ended. I'd been hesitant anyway when I awoke that morning. With a layer of sleep dividing me from the events of Monday, they had become like a dream – strange, interesting, a concern, perhaps cathartic, but soon enough buried beneath subsequent events, if I allowed it. That's why I was partly glad when I failed to find Laura in the morning, because I knew that gradually my zeal for the whole thing would fade. I did not want a secret life. At this stage I could still have returned to my old job, claiming ill health. It would have been cowardly but I might yet have found a way to prefer my old unhappiness. I was also sure that many men liked looking at Laura, and I did not like the thought. I won't say that her shape or her smile had no pleasurable effect on me, but I wanted more than those. It was my hope that she and I would share something, so I needed to know there was a path towards it. I decided to give her all my efforts for one more day.

So Wednesday I arrived at dawn and this time saw her leave almost immediately. The salon where she worked was in the financial district and opened early for morning trade. Thenceforth I had no hope of losing her, and indeed it became quite pleasant to sit in the cafe opposite over the weeks that followed. I read a lot. I have always read a lot. I also pretended to be writing at my computer, and as a result did write a few screwy essays. You might expect this period to find me out at last, as my new life became routine. I think I expected that myself, but it didn't happen. My plate-glass windows, hers, that road between us, tea. It was a daily delight to sit and watch Laura and her colleagues.

She was the salon junior, which meant she clocked a lot of broom time, but when she did cut hair she was quick and confident, and chatty with her clients' reflections. There was more of that laughter, inaudible this time, and she had a nice way of grinning and clutching sections of her own hair to demonstrate choices, a great compliment to most clients, making them feel they qualified for the comparison. Nevertheless I formed the impression that Laura was not happy. The chattiness vanished with her colleagues, a surprise given her adeptness socially and all the lulls. More often she'd read her phone, or go outside and talk on it. In short, she gave off little eagerness for anything but distraction until she had a customer. At lunchtime in good weather she brought in sandwiches. When it rained she got some from a cafe – not, fortunately, my own. She'd leave the salon to eat, come what may. It was rare to see her share even a cup of something with the others. She seemed elsewhere in a number of ways.

I considered it but I never did go in to have her cut my hair. It would have been a hard thing to make seem natural, I knew, though making the decision stick was just as hard. Over and over I called the matter closed, each time finally, but soon I'd catch myself again imagining the feel of that seat, her fingers in my hair, rehearsing the routes our talk might take from being young to being busy to freelance work to private clients and their big houses . . . In the end I shaved my head to shut temptation away.

I knew, you see, and it is one thing my instincts have been right about from the beginning, that if I talked to her everything would change. After that she'd see me. It's hard when you get stuck, and I was stuck with Laura for longer than I'd tolerate these days. It's not the waiting itself that's hard, it's knowing that one quick conversation could deliver the answer. It's hard not to think about that pretty much all the time, which drives you crazy. These days I generally adopt what you might call a fatalist attitude. Let what will happen happen. If somebody else appears and I want to give up on a subject, I give up. Back then I had it yet to learn that other subjects would appear. Back then I did not know that there would *be* other subjects. Now I enjoy switching. I've got quite breezy about it. You know you can always go back to someone later if they stay in your mind. It became a great pleasure, after the first couple of years.

The point is that accosting a subject has to be the last

resort. You can discover much indirectly, if you're cunning. Try this for instance. Approach somebody who knows the subject well. Choose someone trusting and garrulous, and say you are sure the two of you have met. Or don't say, if you have the nerve. Just act like you expect to be remembered. Increase the awkwardness until they ask to be reminded how you know each other, and at this point say you met at the subject's birthday party once, or in a bar with them, or at a conference with them, or at university with them. Whatever you think suits the situation. The important thing is that they hear you use the subject's name and give correct details about them, establishing that the subject is your mutual friend. In my experience this will be enough to make them tell you, in answer to your question, how the subject is these days. Above all be confident. Because you can be confident. A hard thing to believe, but true. Remember that your real motives, however uneasily they sit with you, will seem impossibly far-fetched to anyone who contemplates them, so people never do. If you're accosted by a subject and actually accused, by the same token they're probably past listening to your stories and it's best just to walk away. I'll talk more about this later.

With Laura the thing that made the difference in the end was a phone call, because she loved a phone call, Laura did. I'd begun letting myself queue behind her at the bus stop, and one time heard her tell an old school friend that she *had a drink with Edward Beasley*. That phrase exactly, with the surname. Not Ed or Ted or Eddie. The odd formality meant either that she and her friend had several acquaintances called Edward, with the result that one of them needed the designation Edward *Beasley*, or that she was referring to a figure of some importance that neither of them knew well. The words *had a drink* also suggested seriousness, as opposed to the more social *went for a drink*, or so it seemed to me. Internet research revealed a film producer called Edward Beasley. I found a photograph of him at an awards event which quite closely matched my memory of the suave mineral water drinker. A few days previously I'd been confused to hear Laura say during another phone call that she'd *had no training*, when I'd already established that she'd completed her hairdressing diploma recently. I therefore began to work with the theory that it was dramatic training that she hadn't had, and was considering, which tallied with how often she went to the cinema, three times in the first nine days I studied her, despite the expense. It was a vindication not only of my patience but of my assiduous record-keeping, without which I'd not have had her past remarks to scan for clues. This is an important principle. Don't write down what seems important. Write down everything.

Because Laura had acting dreams. I won't make this more mysterious than it is. She'd taken delight in plays at school but never told her parents how much delight, and instead told herself that drama college was expensive. It's not that they were tyrannical, Mr and Mrs D, not in the least. Laura spoke only kindly of them, that I heard. But they were stiff-minded. I followed them shopping one Saturday afternoon and you could see from their obedience to their list that these weren't people who dove into life off the high board. (Why else are there steps down into the water?) *We're afraid that you'll lose interest in it*, I expect Laura believed her mother would say about acting, after conferring with her father, a softened version of their real fear, that acting would lose interest in her. And so, part-pragmatist herself, I'm sure she'd skipped the whole encounter and resolved to give defeatism a chance, which for a while meant waitressing, then for a while longer, with travel and university intentions that just would not set. Because dreams are seeds. They're growing machines that will not stop unless you break them. And the young have not had time to learn this. So Laura's life stalled, as lives often do at twenty-two, before stalling's fatal. She accepted hairdressing college at her parents' suggestion and expense, and for a time her higher hopes abated.

I like to imagine Laura serving the canapés when she heard Edward Beasley give advice to a young actor at an industry event. It would have been during her waitressing years, and she would have lingered all she could, offering and re-offering rabbit croquettes to everyone within ear-shot, which perplexed a few in that dense crowd. At last with her tray empty she returned to the kitchen and thought no more of it, but she could not forget *Edward Beasley* from the badge. There would have been many months of gloomy toying with the name until she emailed him. I did admire Laura for that, perfumed Laura, going so far off her turf to ask about getting into movies. I don't know what she thought awaited her in the pub, but she was ready for anything, I think, except the anticlimax that she found. Besides getting work as an extra, which she knew led nowhere, Beasley had only drama college to recommend. Expensive indeed, if she were accepted, on top of the debt for learning to cut hair. Plus twenty-three was kind of late.

Had things gone differently Laura might have made an actor. That's my view. Because not once did she visit the cantankerous lady client during the weeks I studied her. I believe she invented the old woman, and her grievances, as a sudden and high-spirited improv piece for her old college mate, and loud enough for an audience of eavesdroppers. The truth was just too true for her to talk about, poor thing. I also believe she wanted to be tactful with a friend still eager about hairdressing. She was a thoughtful girl, more than you'd think, a born considerer of feelings.

I still visit Laura on occasion and she still cuts hair, already more of a Cézanne. Time was I went often, but I moved on a bit, then she moved too, some miles away in fact, in search of better pay she told her mum and dad, but I think just wanting a flat of her own to audition husbands in. She knows nothing of me. It's fanciful, I know, but I think of myself bringing comfort to her with my notes on the death of her dream. I can't make her happy, but I can know that someone is watching and saying, *I'm here, Laura. I understand.*

It is not Laura that I need to tell you about, however. It's Frances. I'm going to take a break. Then I am going to try.

FRANCES B IS AWAKE. Sunlight glows in the curtains but she hears no alarm. Did she silence it and forget? She never wakes so calmly, and this is a big day. In a frenzy she checks the clock but no, it is early. She's been woken early by nerves. She lies back and extends her legs through the sheets into cool new regions. It's like being lowered into a deserved bath of relief.

The alarm sounds. She pulls off her pyjamas and stands with a finger in the shower waiting for heat. She is not overweight, but recently had an attack of optimism and before showering tried morning runs. She bought an expensive pair of shoes, like other people's. She loves their science, their sprung seriousness. She loves their height. (She isn't tall.) Altogether she has worn them three times, not counting in the shop. Three times she pushed through the cold of the day's first mist until she was hot. While she ran she thought about work, then about work and running, then only about running, then about when the running would stop. She imagined giving birth would be a bit like this. Three times was plenty.

Wet from the shower she trembles even in her towel.

There's no heating because her housemate Stephanie insists they do not need it in the mornings, seeing as how they are both gone by eight. This is rich coming from Steph who half the time stays at her boyfriend's.

Frances slips on tights, a yellow blouse and a charcoal suit she likes but which she knows she overwears. In the kitchen she tidies away the remnants of a traditional paella, according to the packet. She half-listens to the radio with tea and reads through the new business pitch she has to do that day. Using her time to work instead of eating cereal will justify later buying a coffee and a pain-aux-raisins. She scoops vile food into the cat's speckled feeding area, as required by the cat. She is – she dreads being asked – a management consultant. It is ten past eight.

The pavement clatters with the shoes of the just washed, all walking to the station. A year ago, when work was not so good, Frances used to get a rutted feeling from the crowd. Now it gives something that is almost joy. She knows that sounds ridiculous. You're meant to moan about commuting, but for her there's some sleepy comradeship in these roads. Some understanding in the way they shiver into motion. *This is how we get things done.*

Steph calls while Frances is queueing at the station cafe. Steph's boyfriend Greg has gone off with her keys, so Frances has to leave a spare under the bin outside. They laugh, she and Steph, about what Steph is like. Frances returns to the house, rummages in the kitchen drawer until she finds the key, then hurries back, not wanting to miss the pain-aux-raisins. On the train she reads a novel and leaves flakes of pastry in the pages.

Passing through the office turnstiles she returns the smile of the security guard. He knows nothing of her triumph at QTel, an overextended telecoms firm whose business Frances helped to stratify, Frances and her team, with calm and convincing demonstrations that they were spending too much on staff, but also with proof of the potential in their high-street units. More potential than Will thought.

Will is her team leader. She likes him enough. At any rate she sees the value that he adds. Clients find it easier to be told what to do by a tall, privately educated man. Will is also a director of the company. She and he are becoming a good combination, and this is becoming known. (Although she does all the work.) (Although this is known as well.) Today they've been assigned the pitch to ComPex, a facilities management firm. She won't actually lead the pitch. She's just written what Will is going to say.

She emerges gratefully from the lift on the eighth floor. She remains not very keen on lifts, but does not let on. Here they work voluntary hours. It's compulsory to call them that. This morning the office is crowded. People lean against the glass walls and chat in the kitchens. Half of them are with clients most days, so they chat when they can. Celia is washing something in the sink and getting a little sprayed. The taps here are ferocious. Celia is probably the best runner, Frances thinks. She runs to work each day before her family are awake. Her hair is dark and flat from showering.

Frances doesn't have her own desk. Nobody does. There are sofas and coffee tables and rows of stools and shelves and basically everything that isn't a desk. The shelves have espresso pod machines that some people are obsessed with.

Bowls of fruit everywhere get secretly replenished. You grab a coffee and some fruit and a bit of shelf, is the idea. You also recommend this way of working to other firms. It stimulates creative exchange, you say. (Although the directors still have offices. There are limits.)

Hi Fran. Do you have a minute?

This is Will now. He's come over before her laptop is even open.

Hi Will, she says. Sure. You feeling pumped? I've just got a few things I'd like you to look at before we go over to ComPex.

Yes, that's what I meant to say.

What?

They've gone with LPP.

Sorry, what?

I got a call first thing. They've already appointed LPP. We've been stood down.

Turned down, this means, but the words are too final for Will, who thinks bad news can be ignored by calling it temporary. It's one way he thinks he is a leader.

You're kidding. Why?

I don't know all the details, just that they liked LPP's proposal yesterday, and did the deal on the spot.

He begins to walk towards his office and she follows.

But they haven't heard ours yet!

I know. I know. Obviously there's wheels within wheels.

They've undercut us, haven't they? They want something in facilities so they've gone in cheap.

Maybe. Probably. If so, it shows they knew they'd have to, which is a real compliment to us. It's a shame though, after all that work. Were you up late?

Yes. I was at QTel yesterday, presenting to staff, but I came back afterwards to finish the pitch. I'd rather have stayed, to be honest. It's going really well at QTel and there were lots of questions.

I'm sorry about that. But look, there's something else I want to talk about.

Oh?

He hauls his door closed. The glass doors are heavy.

It's strange, but we've had a bit of an odd email.

A what?

An odd email. About your work at QTel.

My work? Who from?

Well that's what's odd. It's anonymous. The whole board was copied in on it late yesterday afternoon. It comes from some random address.

What does it say?

He hands her a copy someone's printed.

It's a real hatchet job basically. About you. Whoever wrote it, they say that since you started at QTel you've been arrogant and rude. As soon as our plan was adopted they say you began hinting that you might go it alone as a consultant, sounding people out to poach the business, basically. There's also talk about fraud, saying you've been inflating your hours and trying to get yourself booked for work that doesn't exist, promising people kickbacks from your bonus. It's strong stuff.

She is staring at the page but can't make sense of it. The words streak by. She begins again, determined to be patient, and the meaning slowly comes.

Will is speaking.

Weird, eh? I've never seen anything like it, and of course I see no reason to believe it either.

You *see no reason* to? Or you just don't?

Well, I've not been with you all the time, so of course . . . But no. It isn't something I'd believe about you. No.

How about the others?

The board?

Yes. What do they think?

Well they'll take a lead from me, I expect. But I've spoken to a couple and from what they already know of you they find this very surprising.

It's not surprising. It's untrue. They do see that distinction? You have *told* them that? This stuff about how I'm going freelance, and the stuff about my hours, it's not a misunderstanding or an educated guess, it's totally made up. They know that, don't they?

Right now that's what everyone is assuming, yes. And we certainly intend to get to the bottom of it. Basically we need to find out who sent this email and what's going on.

Come on, Will! Someone has a grudge for some reason. Someone at QTel doesn't like what we're doing and they want to stir things up. Maybe they lost their job. Maybe they got divorced. Maybe they're a drinker.

But why pick on her? That's what even the shelves are asking. Something startles birds off a roof outside. Will says,

I'm sure this is a shock to you.

Well it would be if it weren't such utter rubbish. It is a bit weird that somebody would do it, yes. But there's never been a shortage of weird people in the world.

No. Quite.

He laughs too much, like he's been wanting to.

Have you asked one of the tech guys to trace it? Did you get the IP address?

We did that this morning.

This unsettles her a little. The speed and efficiency of this.

They say it's muddled by a VPN of some kind, but it probably did originate at QTel.

OK.

Can you think of any QTel employees who might have a problem with you? People did lose their jobs because of what we recommended.

People did, it was true. But is this how they would react? QTel had been an unusually open and cheerful project, and yesterday an especially cheerful day. Redundancies had been expected long before Frances came to recommend them, and were expected in greater numbers than she achieved. Plus almost all were voluntary. This is something that Will knows, the client knows, everybody knows. This is something that the client specifically expressed gratitude for in a message to the board that mentioned her by name.

No, she says.

Will is doing his kind face.

Here's what I suggest. The ComPex pitch isn't happening now, sadly. And like you say, this is pretty weird news. I'd definitely find it hard to concentrate. So I suggest you take the day off. Work from home, and don't bother too much about the working. Maybe rerun who you met at QTel and jot down some names. Try to remember any conversations you had that might have triggered something. Then come back in tomorrow so we can straighten it all out. The rest of the team don't know anything yet. If they ask, I'll just say you went home after we lost the pitch.

We didn't lose the pitch. We never did it.

You know what I mean.

She looks at him. At his height, at his haircut. It might be good advice to go home, although she doubts it comes from caring. Three small girls smile from the frame on his desk, bunched along the back of a horse that also doesn't care. She must not cling here spitefully. Not if that's the reason. She has told clients many times, and it is true, that the most successful businesspeople are the ones who can defy their pride. So it is meekly that she takes her dead pitch back to the lift, then back to the station where the renovations and improvements never end. And gradually she starts to think, on the one functioning escalator, on the train, on the streets of home, blithe now with crocodiles of schoolchildren, hearty with the sounds of building and of builders . . . She thinks, *Am I in trouble here?*

The email isn't crazy. Sat on the sofa in her living room she has read it many times. Controlled, that's what it is. Direct yet calmly phrased. No lurid idiosyncrasies or solecisms and enough rhythmic variety to imply some thoughtfulness behind the serious claims, but not imply pleasure being taken in them. There is a relaxed attitude to cliché and an infinitive left split. Altogether the impression is of a person who is good at writing and probably good at several things. The author seems familiar with her work at QTel and with consulting generally. The only false note is the central allegation, that a junior consultant has been plotting to poach clients from her firm, a laughable idea frankly, and she expects the board's been laughing. So why is she not reassured? Time and again she pulls herself back from the brink of believing that she did indeed, at some point, give somebody the wrong idea. She notices herself presuming that the author is a man, and can't dismiss the feeling. On a whim she sends an email from her own address saying only, *Who is this?* Then she regrets it.

She is still wearing her coat, and goes to hang it in the hall. Without it she is cold, so on her return she bends down – not easily in her work skirt, she'll change – to heap up logs and firelighters in the grate. From the doormat she fetches a handful of pizza leaflets and positions them as fuses. She gets round them all with a single match before her fingers scorch. Kneeling on the carpet she raises her palms to the growing flame.

Is there someone at QTel? Someone odd she's noticed? She tries making a list of names, but none convince her. Of course if the claims were true she might well know who sent the email, because she'd know who she had plotted with. She'd be angry with this person for sabotaging her plans but would not want to name them, because then they would be free to accuse her openly. If she were guilty she would probably just act baffled, name no one, and hope that the affair would fade away. The fire is too hot for her knees. She stands.

She should relax. Hard problems are rarely solved with

a direct approach. She lies on the sofa and switches on the television. Nothing good is on so she watches nothing good for a while.

Later she thinks, *Will did it*. Will did it. He might not have sent the email himself, but he could have connived with somebody at QTel. Some ally from one of those meals without her. Will or the ally sent the email from an office computer, and Will would see to it that they weren't caught. Maybe he sabotaged the ComPex pitch as well, not wanting to credit her with winning it? Maybe he thinks her success is a threat to him? Maybe it is? She changes her mind. This is conspiracist nonsense.

She's drowsing in the bath when her phone rings.

Hi Steph, she says.

Hi Fran. Sorry to bother you at work.

Ah! But I'm not at work!

You're not?

No. Hear that?

She whisks the water with her fingers.

What is it?

I'm in the bath!

You're in the bath?

I am.

She wonders where all this levity has come from.

Why are you in the bath?

I came home early. It's all a bit odd. Someone at QTel has been complaining about me to Will. To the whole board actually. They wrote an email saying I've been defrauding the company and trying to poach clients in order to set up a consultancy of my own.

Have you?

Stephanie! Of course I haven't!

Jo-king! It's just Jo King again. Who wrote it?

It's hard to tell with anonymous emails, Steph. When I find out you'll be the first to know.

Shit. Well that's horrible, Fran. Are you OK?

I think so. I mean it's obviously not nice. And it's sad because everything seemed to be going so well when I was at their office yesterday. I gave a report to the staff and answered questions, and people seemed happy with the new system. They'd really begun to feel like it was theirs, you know? I guess that only alienates the dissenters even more, feeling the tide turn against them. Perhaps that's what drove somebody to this. In the end, I don't see how one mad email could become a big problem, but I do want to work out what's going on.

Has the bath helped?

Not really. I doubt it's complicated. Obviously I pissed someone off without realising it, and they're a bit strange, and they sent this email. The company can't sack me just for that. Not without getting sued anyway.

It's pretty scary though, the idea of someone out to get you. Are you sure you're OK?

Yeah, I'm fine. I'm more pissed off about planning for a pitch that didn't happen, to be honest. That's another thing. That's why I came home.

The big one you were talking about?

Yes. They went with someone else and cancelled the meeting.

Poor you! You're having a rotten day.

Yeah. Not great.

Well look, I'm coming home myself soon, so we can talk properly then. Are the keys still where you left them?

Shit, I forgot. Yes they are.

Great, thanks. It feels like ages since I saw you.

Steph is the third housemate. She is a replacement for Annie, who was a replacement for Marina, but there'd been the most jollity when Steph moved in. Old university friends, or at least friends of friends, the two of them straight away found much to laugh about, much more than expected. They laughed about Steph's clumsiness. They laughed about Annie's hypochondria and promiscuous belief in remedies. They laughed reliably and regularly, about whatever was to hand, and the laughter bound them as friends as sex binds lovers. They laughed about being nearly the last single women they knew, and about the crazy revenge they'd take on being abandoned for a man. It was a classic prisoner's dilemma, Frances said, then explained game theory.

Greg is a lawyer and Stephanie's boyfriend, the eventual graduate from a parade of flings. He is structurally difficult for Frances to like, because he threatens to take away both Steph and her mortgage payments. These feel like selfish grievances, so Frances is also structurally disposed to find fault with his character, and as it happens the man's preening misogyny and controlling nature are plain to anyone who looks with open eyes. This is not Stephanie, however. She talks a lot of neoplatonic claptrap about the true, ideal Greg that only she can see.

Steph is a children's entertainer, not successful. She offers franchised toddler music lessons that haven't caught on.

Even so her rent has been very prompt lately, and Frances wonders whether Greg has begun shielding his girlfriend from the market. It would explain her willingness to forgive his long and unpredictable hours, even to feel grateful for them. She would be ashamed of this fact, but Frances has never dared to raise it. For more than a year she has waited for the return of the true Steph, but her hopes are wavering. It is sad but calming, to lose hope. It reduces her emotional exposure.

See you soon then, babes.

Steph jokingly calls people *babes*. The joke is about people who do it without joking.

Yeah. See you soon.

Frances has no boyfriend, which works well. The point was tested in the summer when she holidayed alone for the first time, not fully by choice, yet took delight in the silent meals spent watching other diners, the reading marathons, the ample but respectful male attention, on the whole. At the beach she seemed to summon a game of football by flinging down her towel. She'd be woken by the scattering of young men's sand across her toes, or calves. Sometimes she'd roll the ball back. Older men were evening specialists, she noticed. They had a way of offering coffee that made vivid what they would really like to give her, and she'd not in principle been opposed to letting one or two, but in the end preferred peace. As a rule she waits for desire to stab sharply before acting, in one or another of the available ways. Overall she would guess, and she has some evidence, that she is more sexually satisfied than any of the married women that she knows.

She wakes up in cold water, hungry. She hooks out the bathplug with a toe and feels the level tugging down. In the fridge she finds a prawn curry with rice, which she pushes out of its sleeve into the microwave. She goes to the boiler, slides the switch to constant and hears the stomp of the gas. The dishwasher needs emptying. The microwave pings. Inside, the food tray is soft and hot. Steam puffs out as she peels away the film. The curry section is edged with bubble holes and the rice section is a block of hissing grains. The latch clicks in the hall. It will be Stephanie.

I'VE BEEN UNCOMFORTABLE with eye contact all my life. I find it like being in a mirrored lift. We look into each other's eyes and suddenly I am looking at you looking at me looking at you looking at me looking at you . . . It's too much. I spin out. But I'm probably oversensitive. Or the reverse. I'm a pachyderm. Hide is a good word for what I'm covered with. That might explain my need to confess.

I first noticed Frances because she was carrying an outsized brick of a bag on her shoulder. It bounced against her hip, making her slender body limp in time. I was in a meeting room on the side wall of a large office. She was in the main space outside. She put the bag on the floor and unzipped it. I could not see what she was doing from where I sat, so I returned to my own business until my attention was caught again by a bent white rectangle of light. It flickered into place before her, half on the far wall, half stretched along the floor. With some fiddling she was able to shift the image upwards, but not far enough. In the end she propped the projector's front feet on its own travel case so that, after a quick zap around the room, the image settled near the centre of the wall. Others looked over from their desks. A man standing beside her made an announcement to them. I could not hear his words through the glass, but they had the effect of gathering a crowd. Some brought pen and paper, some trundled their chairs along like pets. She must have had a remote control in her hand, because the image on the wall changed. *Consent,* it said in large navy letters, and in small ones in the corner *QTel Delivery 3*. Below that was her email address.

By this point maybe forty people were waiting, maybe eighty or more. There was a cheer when she began to speak, which swelled when it was realised that cheering was allowed. This startled my meeting, and the people with their backs to the glass turned round. There was some explaining, then we returned to the matter at hand. The others did. Someone asked me what the ultimate unit cost would be if we scaled up. They only wanted a ballpark figure but I had to be asked three times.

The crowd must have been struggling to see her as much as I was, because a small table was dragged over, on which eventually, with an uncertain smile, she agreed to stand. That got another cheer, ignored this time by those around me, and from her platform with flushed cheeks she began. *Consent* was a flexible working structure newly applied to the business, and it was succeeding. She and the new structure were popular anyway, and when she was done they clapped her down. Some who were finishing notes had to clap one-handed against their thighs or notepads. Some stayed to ask questions. Packing up the projector she was badgered on all sides. I too was being asked things again, but by then I was no longer listening, nor cared to pretend.

———

I could easily have missed her. That's what I dwell on, alone here in the dark, exhausted, my flask of tea gone cold, writing this. What if I had missed her?

I was able to discover that she was a consultant, and where she worked, but of course I didn't know that she would come. I was in the Rising Sun, the pub opposite her office, a fine rectangular brass boozer, stripped floorboards, big as a barn, windows from the waist up and old photographs of itself on the walls. It was only a Monday afternoon but the place was filling. I sat at my window table for a long time listening to the other drinkers.

One guy – young, not thirty – he had girlfriend trouble. I could not quite see him, but I heard clearly. He and another man got straight to it when they were settled with their drinks, this chat he'd planned. There was a gap, he said, a chasm that was growing. She had annoying habits. Just habits, but annoying. He'd not brought them up because he worried it was picky of him to mind but now, he said, just four months into this relationship he'd yearned for, she was already dwindling in his feelings. The mate listened, in his way. Rise above it, he said. Women, he said. There were a few pats on the shoulder, offered timidly as though to a wild animal, lest too much sympathy tip the man into sobs. You had to wonder whether the first man was a poor judge of confidants or just not rich in friends. You couldn't exclude the possibility that he had his own annoying habits. Anyway, I reached below the table for my notebook to record some of this, and as I rose I saw her. Waiting at the kerb, hair tossed by the wind, a soft-shouldered tiredness, but absolutely Frances.

When a gap in the traffic appeared she burst across. Clutching my bag, I pushed through sheets of drinkers and just made it to the door in time to see her vanishing into a small supermarket along the way. I could so easily have missed her.

Taking the basket after hers I went up the adjacent aisle at barely a saunter, my blood loud. I passed sugar, eggs, flour, baking materials and tinned goods before stopping to consider some instant porridge. She stood at the chiller cabinet on my right, holding a green prawn curry and a traditional paella from the super-premium range. She read the labels and in the end put both in her basket with an overpriced Chablis, the most expensive white wine available chilled, I established, and probably therefore either a present or a celebration, most likely for herself given the time, which was nearly ten. Queueing with my porridge I watched her operate the automatic check-out, which she did with smooth familiarity, not hunting for buttons. With the shopping and two black bags, one slung over her shoulder, she looked quite burdened on the walk to the station. Nevertheless she went some way along the platform, to where I presumed the exit at her station would be. Despite the train being only two minutes away, she sat down and pulled a paperback from her bag and was soon absorbed enough for me to stare safely. The mist of down on her calm skin, her eyes' busy processing of the type. She was so absent in one way, so fiercely present in another. Truly reading is a variety of sleep. No other memory of the night has stayed so livingly.

After watching maybe unwisely long, when the train came I considered it good policy to join a different carriage. I got glimpses through the jostling window frames, and when she took off her coat I knew we would be on a while. Trains are my turf. I've had years of practice on them. For instance, I know that if you spend time looking at the map then you are planning or measuring your remaining journey and therefore unlikely to be going anywhere routine, like work or home. She did not glance at the map, nor even at the passing platforms, and we went through many stations. I expect I was tired as well. I admit I did lose some alertness. My notes say that she sat near a woman with a polythene-covered tray of leftover sandwiches on her lap, but I have no memory of that. Then at one stop, in that slack pause after the passengers had got off and on, she just grabbed everything and ran. The doors were already closed when I realised. Had I been spotted? This was my first concern, but pretty soon I decided that I hadn't. She'd got lost in her book was all, and saw where she was just in time. I watched her standing on the platform, reaching up through her coat sleeves. The train gears engaged. The roll began and she approached the exit, which was indeed right there.

I hope I'm not making this sound easy? This isn't easy. With practice I've overcome many technical problems in my work, it is true, but many other problems still stand before me, the moral and philosophical problems mostly, which as the years advance cast longer shadows in the mind. I try to escape them by declaring rules, or laws, or principles. Essentially I want to renounce my right to change. In the end, though, all my rules become brittle, friable, woodwormed with exceptions.

I try to remind myself that discovery in general need not be a happy business. Einstein was as prodigious a discoverer as there's been, yet he spent years opposing Minkowski's conception of spacetime, as derived from his own special theory of relativity, before finally adopting it. For years more, he insisted that the universe was static, despite having helped to prove it was expanding. One may achieve great things reluctantly, is the point, with all one's efforts pushing the other way.

When I started out, for instance, I had that rule I've mentioned about not making contact with my subjects or influencing their lives. This was part practical, to avoid detection, but the larger part was ethnographic, because I had the notion that what I witnessed would be inauthentic if contaminated by my fingermarks. Then the exceptions came. The first was a divorcee called Carmen G, my eighth subject and most longstanding at the time. At the end of a marriage begun too young, Carmen had embarked on a dating campaign, seems the best word, and hurrying to make an assignation one evening left her phone on the train. I saw it when she stood up, wedged sideways into the top of the gap between her seat cushion and the carriage wall. In normal life I would instantly have returned the phone, but was this normal life? I was only there because she was my subject, after all, and I had my rule, which meant leaving the phone where it was. It was a crowded train, however. Had I not been in my seat, somebody else would have been, and that person might have spotted the phone and given it back to her, which would make it interfering on my part *not* to. The chance was small, but it was not negligible. No matter what I chose therefore, even if I didn't influence Carmen's behaviour on this occasion, I wouldn't *know* that I hadn't. This was just the beginning of my confusion. What if I were not the only person in the carriage who was studying Carmen that day? What if somebody less scrupulous than myself was engaged in a project similar to my own and *they* picked up the phone and gave it back to her? What then? According to my rules that would contaminate their project but not mine, which seemed ridiculous. How could the same data be accurate in the hands of one person but not another's? What if I saw this other researcher try to steal her phone? Would it be my duty to prevent them? What if they got close in the crush as we disembarked and, in a bold experiment, put a hand up Carmen's skirt? That would be interference by any standard, but would Carmen's reaction, whatever it might be, remain authentic in my eyes? I was having relativity problems of my own. What if the person groping Carmen had somehow heard about my project, and done so for my benefit? Would this be OK if I did not know? I still worry quite a bit about this, but I think I did learn from the Carmen experience that it is better to relax and try to accept whatever judgements seem right at the time. The phone I delivered to Lost Property.

So I've more or less given up on rules, though that isn't to say I'm wanton. Just a few weeks ago I was studying Amelia P, subject eighty-three. Like Laura, Amelia lived with her parents, but unlike Laura she was seldom there, being consumed most evenings and weekends by a devotion to her job that quite defeated my attempts to understand it. She underestimated herself, I suppose, yet this came with an industrious nature. As a result she was often surprised by her success. Without question she could have become more than a suburban branch manager for a mobile phone company, yet this she seemed glad to be. Excited even. You only had to see her bounce through the mornings, or watch how tenderly she inspected the shop's display units, smoothing a dog-eared poster like the collar of a child. So many hours she spent in that shop and not in the world. And for such little pay. It occurs to me now, but didn't then, that there is a resemblance between the affirmative self-denial of overwork and the bitter pleasure taken in thinness by anorexics. In that sense perhaps it wasn't the job itself that Amelia loved so much as having work to do, which suggests some sorrow she was running from, and foretells her being caught. She was also short, Amelia. Short enough to make *petite* a euphemism, so perhaps that was mixed in there. She often mentioned it. I don't know. I broke all my rules with Amelia, loose as they were. We spent quite an amount of time together. There were moments I wondered if she might be interested in me.

It began when I visited the shop about six weeks ago

and started talking to her colleague Rav about a contract, a new mobile phone contract, meanwhile looking around for somewhere suitable to drop a wallet I had fitted with a recording device. (I'll talk more about equipment later.) The plan, not one I'd tried before, was to leave the wallet where it would be found by the staff after I had left, in the hope that it would stay in the back office until I returned and there gather information about Amelia. Carelessly, however, I had brought the wallet loose in a bag with several other items, and in my haste to fetch it while Rav was looking for a demonstration handset I allowed the contents to spill out. When Amelia first saw me I was scooping two lengths of cable back into a holdall. Together we reached for the UHF transmitter at my feet.

Here's something I have learned: any lie can be made more digestible by mixing it with two parts truth. When caught looking furtive, therefore, the trick is not to claim innocence but to account for your actions in a way that accounts for the furtiveness as well. Be honest about your feelings, which you can't hide, but obscure their cause. I remember being accosted at a motorway service station by a subject who returned from the toilet early with her baby son to find me trying to fix a microphone to the underside of her banquette. After some feeble bluster on my part, I'm sure, I sighed and said that I was in fact a private investigator being paid to collect evidence on a man believed by his wife to be an adulterer, and that it was his habit to meet his mistress here. Amused, the subject insisted that she was not here to meet anybody's husband. I said I knew that, but hadn't known the table was occupied. She was so delighted by the story that I don't think she even considered not believing it. In the end I had to deter her from staying to watch the man arrive.

So I was a private investigator again. That's what I told Amelia, and laughed that I perhaps wasn't a very good one, and she laughed too. She asked about my work. Was the shop being investigated? No, I said. I just needed a phone. Investigators need lots. We talked, and soon I felt her purpose. The company, she said, had a regular problem with clients who disappeared without paying their bills, not only at this branch but nationally. The sums owed were rarely large, so it was rarely worth the cost of tracking down the debtors singly. Together, however, the debts amounted to a lot. Some were chased for the sake of appearances. She was willing to be candid about that. But as the rest were too small to sell to collection agencies they were generally written off. The company had non-payment insurance, but that itself was expensive, and worth it only because it made the losses more predictable, taking the sting from the extreme years. On its own this might have been a bearable expense, but concern was now filtering down from the top that it might get known they were soft on debts, and that this might attract a lower class of client, which might in time bring down the brand. Each year branch managers were made to be more stringent about new clients' paperwork and credit ratings. They'd even had to refuse some renewals. Marketing denied it, but she also thought she saw this snobbery in the drift towards firmer pricing, which was emptying the shop and draining morale. I tried not to show surprise that she was telling me all this, as we perched on stools, her head hardly at my chin. As she went on to say, she had an idea.

People who disappeared without paying their phone bill would not in fact be difficult to find, she guessed, if you knew what you were doing. Having found them, she also guessed, you would often find that they had not paid other debts as well. If so, the cost of tracking down feckless clients might be defrayed by selling their contact details on to other creditors, or to a debt consolidation company. Indeed your non-paying clients might actually turn out to be a profitable asset, as long as you had the idea first. To test this, you'd just need a list of absconders, a capable investigator, and the cost of a few trial runs. She was wasted in a mobile phone shop, as I say.

And she was nearly right. Head office hired me for three days and I was supplied with a list. Many people I found in a few minutes on social media, and induced them to deliver me their details with simple lures. Wiser ones I had to get through friends. One was dead. Most of the rest were hidden only by the effort it took to search through public documents or the electoral roll. They were not exactly catburglars, as Amelia guessed. It was just their way to run.

At the end of a week, forty-one out of the fifty names had addresses next to them. I was a pretty good private investigator, it turned out. On my own initiative I approached a handful, and was at first startled by how easily they yielded. You just explain the situation, usually, and like a ripe tomato the money drops. A few were even grateful, I would say. They told stories that were too long about being slow with paperwork, but you could see their relief to leave behind the worrying, even if it made them poorer. My firm smile was never as bad as what they'd dreaded. That's how it is with the inevitable. It gets remembered in advance and as a result makes bathetic entrances. Think how tamely even death is met by the old. Some of the debtors got almost chirpy. You'd see the brave buds of hope on them again. It was terribly happy and terribly sad, especially knowing that I'd sell their details to their other creditors.

I was asked to go to head office to help Amelia with her presentation and answer questions. It worried me, but I agreed. And she did a fine job in there. No way was her proposal rejected for any flaws in its performance. The one thing she lacked, which you'd expect maybe, was street smarts. She didn't understand that she was saying to her superiors, *I've thought of something that you should have thought of first*. Plus I've admitted that my attention wandered. Several times I was caught staring at my laptop and through the glass. She looked like she'd stepped from a commercial, Frances with her work clothes and her incidental beauty, her command over the crowd. No question but she caught the eye. After a while what occupied me more, though, were the men and women she was speaking to. They smiled in the projector light, smiles held ready to burst into cheers or laughs. Men in their fifties gazed like boys. She wasn't winning them over with words or technique. These people were already won. They knew her. They trusted her. I'd never seen anything like it. I wondered what made her special. I wondered how it must feel to be so loved, and by so many, to have people wanting you all to themselves. Some staked their claims by heckling. I couldn't hear what was said but you could see when Frances met them with ripostes, when with embarrassment. Both ways the room was charmed and the cheers and laughter broke, ruffling our meeting.

The guy who was in charge told us he was sorry about the distractions, but I think he meant that it was I who ought to be. I don't like being admonished and in a loud plain voice accepted his apology. Then I excused myself, folded my laptop, and took it to the toilet. I must have lingered too long in the crowd afterwards, because when I returned the meeting was over. Amelia stood alone by the door. *They said thanks for coming,* she said without a smile. Days later when she confirmed the bad news by phone she was angry. Really angry. I'd not heard her even grumble before. It worried me how she'd take this setback, but by then I was busy with other worries, as you will see.

Did Frances stir my nerves in a new way? They always do, but I'd never gone so far. Mainly I think that things between us developed, although the fact that I don't know is interesting. I know I often had second thoughts early on. Now she is such a part of me that our first encounters feel ancient and unalterable, even though they only happened weeks ago.

These are my initial notes.

l20s/e30s, slim, straight br hair, av height, attractive, mgmt conslt (esp IT, tech and telecoms?), generally liked, Consent, prob long hours, def well paid, graduate, confident, low socmed activity, no w ring

That's it. I must have been tired. I usually write more. Yet there I was at her station early the next morning, waiting. I waited a long time, being loyal and being used to it and knowing the moods. When she arrived she didn't come straight to the platform, but began queueing at the cafe outside. I saw her through the fence. Had I been standing closer to the rails she'd have been hidden by the crowd. Soon afterwards she took a phone call, and as I made my way down she left. I took out my own phone and pretended to be talking to a wife about a nanny while Frances led me to a late-Victorian terraced street. Speed bumps, small trees, dog turds, tight mortgages. No houses were grand, but hers was among the loved, its windows clean, its tiled path swept and weeded. I walked on until I was nearly out of sight, then stopped to hunt irritably for something in my bag. She entered the house and quickly re-emerged with a single brass key, bare and glinting, that she slotted away beneath the dustbin before heading back the way she came. I thought about following, then watched her go.

—

The next thing I remember is the smell of the house. That essence of her. This is crazy, I know, but it was familiar. Like coming home after a long trip. I stood in the hall for some minutes taking it in. I'd never been into a subject's home before. I suppose it was an epiphany or something. I've been trying to describe it for a while, and I've taken breaks, but I don't think I can get there on my poetical resources, so I'll just say this: it was less like a dream come true, more like paradise remembered. Does that make sense? Oh well. Sense-making isn't all that it's cracked up to be.

In the front room I found bookshelves and scanned the spines. Most were good quality novels, including many classics. Here and there I spotted crumpled works of theory, which I took to be old university texts. At first I held back from touching anything, but soon I was leafing through them all. Young Frances had written her name inside a history of the Great Depression, pencilling the margin with neat little remarks. If the shelves were arranged with any system, I could not perceive it. Some sections were alphabetised. All the Kafka was together, next to Keynes and Doris Lessing, but then came Margaret Atwood and a pristine foot of Proust. It was perhaps the wreckage of a system not yet put back in order after redecoration, or a move.

Clearly no children lived in the house. Only womenswear hung in the hall. Upstairs there was a bathroom, a loft hatch and two bedrooms, one large, where more books were piled against the wall. The kitchen at the back of the house was neat and tidy, the garden rather overgrown. Drips on the window marked where the kettle had fogged it, and a teabag lay tepid in the bin. Beneath it I recognised the paella packet. The green curry was still in the fridge, the Chablis in the door, about a glass down, beneath a squad of sauce jars. There was also milk, eggs, a gnarled ramp of cheddar and a packet of capsicum traffic lights missing the red.

After opening one cupboard I opened them all. They were not very full of ingredients, but did contain a large amount of crockery, much of it quite old and fancy, and in all far more than two housemates could need. Counting it up, I found two whole dinner services for eight, one a reproduction willow pattern, the other red and white with a gold band. The way all the pieces were just shuffled together in stacks suggested that neither set was kept for best. Combined they would lay the little kitchen table four times over. It was absurd. No one would buy a new set for a house already equipped with the other, so one or both was probably inherited, and valued, and when they came together neither woman had given ground. It might have been a point of wry dispute between them. It might be a cold war. Certainly if either of them really valued her china she could care for it much better in a box until it was ready to preside in the family home for which it was surely intended. Instead it looked like something was being asserted behind the cupboard doors. You imagined Frances using her plates, then her housemate retaliating.

I was back upstairs when I heard the front door open and shut. Then I heard nothing. I had quite lost track of time.

I edged on to the landing and peered through the bannisters, then sprang back, grasping the rail to steady myself. She was in the hall, collecting the junk mail. I hurried into her room, put an ear to the floor and listened. I wasn't really thinking. You blunder around urgently in a crisis because your body is full of adrenaline and above all you want to act. You have to notice this and take yourself in hand. You have to gather up your choices. The sash windows in her room were locked, and in any case offered only a public drop on to the tiled path below. I wanted to run – just run – and there was little to stop me, but even if I was not seen she would surely hear and call the police. I wasn't wearing gloves or anything. On the other hand waiting in her bedroom for a better opportunity risked a confrontation, the worst outcome of all.

Slowly I stepped back on to the landing. The scent of smoke was in the air. The bathroom window was probably too small to escape through, and she might visit the toilet while I tried. She'd be unlikely to visit the other bedroom though, the housemate's. Moreover the window in there was large enough for me to crawl through, once the lock was undone, and the drop would be on to grass. Of course I would then have no escape but the neighbouring gardens, where my problems might multiply. On the other hand if she passed the other bedroom on her way to the toilet, I'd have a clear run to the front door.

So I waited there. If I peered through the hinges I could see the front door, but I made myself wait. I would be out in five seconds, but I made myself wait. It wasn't long before I heard the approach of footsteps, lively and unsuspicious footsteps it seemed to me. They passed by up the stairs. Peering again, I saw Frances in her bedroom. The door was wide open but the curtains were drawn. She was in her underwear, dropping the last of her work clothes into a laundry basket. She put on blue jeans, a white lace camisole and a cerise cardigan, then passed my door again on the way back down.

Hours I waited this time, ever on the tip of running. The housemate was called Stephanie. Her name was written on a large number of bank and other documents scattered on the desk at my side. Apart from these, a small wardrobe and a futon, the room contained nothing but sewing equipment and the things that Stephanie was making. Not curtains or fine dresses, but outlandish big-eyed costumes for the most part, with slots for your real eyes. Those that were not hung on hooks were jumbled in piles. Many were just fragments. Green feet or purple tails. There were glue tubes and bits of tape and cotton reels and putty everywhere. On the hook nearest me hung a rather impressive Loch Ness monster, made out of *blue velour*, my notes say. A cat slept on a pile of offcuts. I unlocked the window, just to be ready.

You know there will be tight spots, doing what I do. I take risk seriously and arrive prepared, but you soon accept that you can't prepare for everything. Some of my best thoughts have been on my feet. Sometimes it's exciting. Not this time. Far too much at stake, and too long to think about it. I gave real consideration behind that door to where my life would go if I got out. I promised myself I'd end the project altogether. Although part of me wanted to be caught. I could feel it. When I imagined her strolling in to borrow something of Stephanie's, and finding me, and thinking on my feet . . . I did not feel fear only. I'd taken things too far with Amelia. Then with Frances I'd taken them further. Now look. This part of me had been waiting for the rest to turn hubristic since the beginning, and the next hours were to be our gleeful denouement. But you can't think like this. That's the voice of obedience. That's what scares people into line. All through these years of my transgression it's been with me whispering, *This won't last, This won't last, This won't last* . . . It makes it hard to plan.

Twice I heard Frances enter the kitchen, but each time held back. When she switched on the television, I opened the door to run, then closed the door again. At last she climbed the stairs, more slowly this time. I heard the bathroom lock engage, the extractor fan begin, the tap crash on. This was my chance, but still I waited. You have to take a calm hold of yourself, as I say. Frances could emerge at any moment. The tap stopped. Then I knew she was in the bath from the echoing sloshes. She would go nowhere quickly. Plus when she began I'd be alerted by the ripping of the water. My chance was ample, now that it had come. I opened the door a nudge, then fully. There was no rush. I approached the bathroom, listening. Her clothes lay on the floor just inside her room. They were still warm.

Her phone rang and I started with fright. She began talking. It was Stephanie. I was halfway downstairs, then stopped again. She was lying in the bath, behind a closed door. She was engaged in a phone call with the only other occupant of the house, who must therefore be at least some minutes away. I heard everything clearly, even on the stairs. How could I not listen? Or not be curious? Why would I pretend? I'd cursed my mischance for a long time, but here it revealed a jewel. I did listen.

Poor Frances. By no means did I want her to undergo the stress of finding me, on top of her other stresses, but I was glad to be there. And I don't know. Not everybody would have noticed it, but I also believe I heard a renewed brightness. The day before, and on the phone this morning, she'd sounded cheerful but as though she was trying. I was sure of it. There was something open in her voice now, and a readiness there. It was subtle. A fresh spirit of inquiry maybe. A project of her own.

I must get back to her.

THE ALARM CLOCK CANNOT BE ringing, but she looks and it is. There was a plan to go in early, she remembers. There was a plan to be ready for anything today.

She pulls the cord in the bathroom and the extractor squeals, then jams, then won't unjam, no matter how she prods it. Soon there will be mould. More mould. She showers with the door and window open, taking her time about it, timorous about leaving the warm water.

She feels appalling. The wine she finished with Stephanie last night has turned her blood to gravel. They talked things through. Progress was made. In the middle her mother rang and became so savagely protective that she needed transfusing with her daughter's calm. Frances went to bed strong, with optimism, but now that's gone like the heat of a clear day.

In the cold she tries to dress too soon. The clothes stick to her wet body and make a nuisance of themselves. Downstairs Stephanie has finished the milk. At least there is no milk. She settles for black tea, doing her makeup while it steeps. It steeps too long and the surface shines with flakes of tannin.

On the train she stares out of the window at the city in the sharp dawn sun. Tries reading but can't. Maybe getting in early is a bad plan. Maybe it will be taken as a statement of something by her bosses. She doesn't want to appear to be making statements. She wants to appear like this whole business is a trifle to her, a whisked nothing, air. Nonchalance is slippery. The harder you grasp at it the faster it flies away.

You're early, the security guard says.

He has a way of just announcing his thoughts. It makes him tend to say things – that it is cold, that she is carrying a lot of bags, that she is working on a Saturday – which they both already know. It is honest at least.

She says,

Morning. Yes. Lots to do.

He murmurs in vague sympathy and seeing her begin to rummage for her swipe card, opens the barrier with his own. This overrides the building's head-count system, which contravenes its fire safety certificate. She says thanks.

The lift is waiting for her. It's that early. And the emptiness of the eighth floor is lavish. The carpet bears fresh comb strokes from the cleaners and their night machines. She takes a low table with a view of the door and pretends to be working in a relaxed way. When Tim appears she almost is.

Morning Fran, he says.

Hi Tim. How's it going?

Good. You're in early.

Yes. I thought I'd try and blast through some bits and

pieces now things are quiet. Will told you about ComPex?

Tim is small and analytical, often amused but never laughing, life a parade of human error, him in the grandstand.

Yes, he says. They undercut us, clearly.

That's what I said.

He looks at her.

And how are you doing?

Well, you know, disappointed. I'm pissed off we did all that work for nothing, but I suppose you can't always win. At least we know they didn't hate the pitch!

I mean after the other thing.

She suppresses a bloom of fear.

Tim says,

The email.

Yeah. That was a bit weird. I don't know what to make of it, to be honest, but I'm sure it will all be sorted out soon enough. Will told you then?

He nods and stares.

Tim isn't much liked around the office. He lacks most kinds of politeness, and all the things you would call charm. In the summer he alone wears sandals, and when deep in work he hums. Hard little riffs, they could be anything really, but they persist for hours. People presume that it's unconscious and say nothing. They share their grievance with exchanged eyebrows and, when he's not there, mimic him. Tim's so good on data centres that the rest of the time they have to be grateful, and he rides around in their gratitude like a Mercedes. He annoys Frances too, but the years defending him have formed a soft spot in her. He acts obnoxious, she believes, in order to avoid discovering whether people like him.

Who do you think sent it? Tim asks.

I really don't know.

Do you have a theory?

I have guesses. But they are just guesses. I haven't been thinking about it all that much. It's not like this person offered any evidence of what they're saying, so I think we just have to ignore them.

Celia comes in blotched pink, nails a workstation with one bag and marches the other to the showers. She's part of a flow of arrivals now. *Morning* dots the air.

Once Tim ordered a prostitute to his hotel room when they were on a training residential.

I see what you mean, he says.

Monica arrives. She is the fourth team member, from Belgium – from the south, she always adds – and perfectly nice. She never minds when people think she's French.

Morning Monica, Frances says. You heard about this email?

Monica nods timidly.

Good. Well I wanted to say, don't worry about it. I have no idea what's going on, but Will is trying to find out. In the meantime I suggest we just ignore it. That's what I'm doing anyway. Unless you have any ideas?

Monica shakes her head and asks,

Are you OK?

I'm fine. Honestly. Thank you.

Frances has tried to be friends with Monica, and continues trying, but whenever they have time together she finds herself babbling, ranging widely across topics, desperate to talk about anything besides the fact that Monica is Belgian, then always arriving back at it. It's got so bad that Monica only has to mention the day's news or a film she's seen to make Frances panic about bringing in Magritte or chips or *Heart of Darkness* or the European parliament. Monica must think she is obsessed with Belgium. Or think she believes that Belgians are. Or think she finds Monica such tepid company that the unremarkable fact of her nationality has become a substitute for her unremarkable character as a whole. This last is of course the most worrying because it's accurate.

I think it has to be one of the QTel execs, Tim is saying. You never know what's happened behind the scenes before we get called in. Someone was probably dead against hiring us. Now they've been proved wrong and they resent it. I expect they've picked on Frances because she's a woman.

They could have picked on Monica, Frances says.

Monica looks hurt instead of laughing.

Anyway, Frances continues. Let Will look into it. I need to talk to him, in fact.

I just saw him, Monica says. He was in the lift, but he kept going up.

This means up to the boardroom, probably. Frances checks, and there is a meeting scheduled. Hours pass. Will does not appear. Frances tries to make her mind stick to other matters. Just before twelve he is by her shoulder.

Hi Fran.

He looks serious.

Oh hi Will. I'm glad you're here. Do you have a minute?

Of course. I was about to ask the same of you.

Tim is wandering their way.

All right Will, he says grinning. Fran's looking for you.

Hi Tim. Yes, I've found her, thanks.

This is how Tim jokes.

My office? Or shall we go get a sandwich?

Office probably.

They walk in silence. Waiting inside with a piece of paper and a glum look is Jenny, the HR manager, Jenny who's really nice and who Frances has drinks with sometimes.

Can I go first? Frances says when the door is closed.

I think it's best if I do.

OK.

So I've had a long chat with the board about you this morning. They've taken a decision, which I opposed, to suspend you on full pay, pending an investigation.

Frances stares.

We need to do it for appearances. That's their view anyway. They value you, and want to bring you back as soon as possible, but they're worried, if the email's even vaguely true, about being seen not to act. I'm not supposed to tell you that officially, but screw it. I'm really sorry, Fran. I know you won't be happy.

She can't think of anything to say.

Jenny looks sad.

Will continues,

Look, some chaps up there are a bit sentimental about the business, basically. They get twitchy about small stuff, like everything's the beginning of the end. They started out by poaching clients from other firms, remember. Now they're terrified of someone doing it to them. The way they see it, if there's even a remote chance you're guilty, then keeping you in the building is a risk.

Will, this is crazy! Am I really suspended?

Yes.

So you can get anybody suspended with one anonymous email?

I know. Believe me, I told them that. Most of them don't have an opinion on whether the email is true, but the fraud stuff on its own is enough for a suspension while we figure it out.

Frances looks at Jenny.

It has to be full pay, Jenny says. But when allegations have been put to the company which might result in criminal proceedings . . .

With zero evidence?

That's what the investigation will establish.

I explained what an asset you were, Will says. But that's not the point. Now they've spent a day worrying, they want it all properly looked into. And to be sure you're not influencing things they want you out of the way.

Unbelievable. This is unbelievable, Will. Are you sure it's not illegal too? Jenny? I'm going to check my contract. Be sure to tell them that.

I'm sure they expect you to.

Was the vote close?

Will gives her his sad eyes.

No. Look, let's go get a sandwich and just talk about this. I know that . . .

I don't want a fucking sandwich, Will! I can't believe

that you're suspending me for doing absolutely nothing. Because of one email with no evidence. One anonymous email means more to the board than all my time here?

Of course not. It's just . . .

Actually, she says. Actually Will, I can't say this surprises me. It was clever of you to send me home yesterday. I'm sure you got all the time you needed.

What?

You understand.

I don't understand, Fran. I was the one saying we should back you. I know you're pissed off but don't lash out at me. I tried everything. Seriously, in your own interests, I'm sorry but calm down.

Thanks. So tell me, were you at QTel yesterday afternoon?

A hand goes through his hair.

What?

When this email was sent, were you there? At QTel?

I didn't send the email, Fran. I had nothing to do with any of this, and I don't want you suspended. I even think you know that, really.

Of course but, you know, since we're investigating this, were you there or weren't you?

Along with about three hundred other people, yes I was. You know I was upstairs.

And if they check back through their network records, will they see that you were logged in when the email was sent?

I don't know what they'll see. I probably was logged in for most of the time. People usually are in offices. Listen,

Fran. I understand you're disappointed, and I'm ready to absorb a bit of emotion here but . . .

She just laughs.

Listen to me, Fran. Listen for a second. I'm going to ignore all of this because I know you and I know you've had some horrible news, but if you start spreading crazy theories. This thing, it may not be a big deal now but that kind of behaviour will make it grow, and maybe then we'll pass a point we can't get back from. And say you're right, OK? Just say you're right and I sent this email, then unless I did something clever with the computer – which you know I can't – then I suppose they'll discover it in the records as you say. Then I'll lose my job, won't I? But if you're wrong, which I think you must accept is a possibility, then you'll be glad that you kept calm.

As will you.

Yes. We'll all be very glad, Fran. You probably don't want my opinion, but actually I think this won't amount to much. The board just want to know what went on with you at QTel. They'll talk to a few people and ask if what the email says is true. They'll find that it isn't, then they'll bring you back, probably give you a present to say sorry, and never forget how well you handled it. Nor will they forget the way I've sung your praises this morning.

Why do Tim and Monica know, Will? Yesterday you said, specifically, that this wouldn't leak out into the office, and what's the first thing Tim says to me this morning?

Sorry, yes, that's a fuck-up. I meant to say. One of the other directors started asking Tim lots of questions yesterday. He basically let the cat out of the bag and I had to explain to both Tim and Monica what was going on so they wouldn't spread it around. I stressed that they must keep quiet, for your sake, so I'm sure they will.

Groups are massing for lunch. A young man stretches in front of the glass.

I'm not leaving.

Listen, Fran.

He goes for an arm around the shoulder. She flinches away.

Listen, Fran. You have to leave. It's ridiculous. I agree it's ridiculous, but you know that there's a protocol in these situations. You have to leave the building.

The sandwich protocol. Of course.

You have to leave, Jenny says.

Will grabs the door handle.

I have no choice, he says.

I'm not moving. I want to talk to the board myself.

They've voted, Fran. I have no choice. Unless you want me to ring downstairs and ask security to escort you out? Would you prefer that? I can do that if you like. And I can print out some bullshit suspension letter for you to take home.

Jenny toys with the paper.

The letter is statutory, Will, she says.

Frances thinks of the security guard coming to get her. She feels sad for him.

Honestly, Frances. On Friday, maybe before Friday, we'll have this whole thing behind us. Will you wait? I'll buy you a very large and very apologetic drink.

No you won't.

She heaves open the door with an exasperated sigh to smother the effort.

On the street she feels the start of tears. She needs somewhere to let them go. People pour past her like floodwaters around a car.

She starts walking, just to be walking, gets up to the pace of the crowd, exceeds it. Her legs go stiffly fast. Her toes stab the world. A small side street opens on her left. There's a cafe a way down. The Rose Cafe. Inside three labourers are queueing. There's a crevassed proprietress and a fat man quietly internalising a roll. She enters and waits in line. When her turn comes she buys tea and finds a window seat with her back to everything. They've taken the laptop, but she has the ComPex pension fund statement in her bag. She props it against the ketchup bottle as a screen. Something about this brings the weeping on, and straight away she knows that they are yesterday's tears. She does her best to regulate them, head on hand, elbow on the table. She might be lost in the columns of data or asleep, were it not for the shaking of her shoulders. In truth she's doing well not to bawl. She wants the world to ring with sorrow. Her work, her joy, her only joy, her grief. How naive she'd been to dream of other outcomes. She's no hotshot. Who has she been kidding? She is a woman in a cafe, crying.

A man enters. He will have seen, but she doesn't care. A well-dressed man in a blue pullover and grey coat, an unlikely patron here, he stands behind her ordering coffee and a doughnut. She takes a napkin from the dispenser and tries to swab away the mess around her eyes. The window is nearly a mirror. The man sits at the table next to her. She knows he's going to lean across the aisle.

Are you OK? I say.

I'M SETTLING INTO THIS, I FEEL, but it has been difficult. I'm always looking back at what I've written and not liking things that I formerly liked, then wondering whether I was right before, or whether I'm right now, and how I can tell, and what constitutes being right anyway, is it reporting only provable facts, or is it being more fully truthful? Often I write about how I felt, or how I feel, then I feel differently. It's confusing but I've accepted now that it won't change. I even welcome it. Confusion seems the right spirit for the task. I was confused at the time.

I'd expect people to disapprove, perhaps you disapprove, but I've never really thought this project was immoral. I work with the presumption that the women I study would be upset if they found out, but if they don't find out, well, where's the harm? The law requires *a negative reaction* in the victim to be proven. Thus it does not protect Frances from being stalked, it protects her ignorance of it, just as it protects other states of ignorance, like childhood or religious faith. My moral duty, if I have one, is to get away with what I'm doing.

This wasn't how I felt behind Stephanie's door, however. Those hours, I'll never forget them. I wanted to feel guilty, and believed I did. I wanted my predicament to be a just punishment for my actions, and thereby hope that the magic of remorse would free me. That's why I was issuing all those sterile vows to change my ways. Besides, I knew I was ready to change. The project had become predictable. My love for it was growing pale.

So I survived that afternoon, but I survived altered. Almost in tears, I returned the key to its place beneath the bin and slipped home through the thinning light. That evening I rested. Like an arthropod following ecdysis, or moulting, this was the soft-skinned period when an animal with a hard exoskeleton may grow. I knew that I was getting governed by events, and I fretted a little. I stared at my table. I went to bed, got up, went back to staring. Two pieces of Stephanie's modelling putty, still squashable, sat there, still bearing the impressions of a key.

It was dark when I got up. I made myself eat porridge. A taxi dropped me at the station and to my surprise she was already there, stamping off the cold at the platform's end. She read nothing on the journey. She seemed tense. Eyes on the window, glancing, eyes on nothing. Her foot jiggled. She checked her phone again. When we arrived I let her walk away. You mustn't dog them just because you don't know what to do.

I rang her office switchboard and asked to be put through to the building manager. I'd started a new sandwich delivery service, I explained. Did they already employ one or did they have a canteen? Sandwiches and a range of salads and sushi boxes, yes, was the answer. No canteen. This improved the odds of seeing her at lunchtime. I like lunchtimes. You get to watch them make decisions. I did some shopping and drank a coffee then settled at a bus stop to wait. When she appeared in the atrium she was with a tall man. Her lips were a line. It didn't look like they were going to lunch. She passed through the door alone, not looking at him, just one bag on the shoulder now. After a few strides she stopped. The crowds were so thick that I thought I'd lost her for a minute. After seeming to consider where to go she headed east at speed, then stopped again at the entrance to a grubby side street, more of an alley really. Just shaded office windows, the entrance to a car park and a dishevelled cafe. Not her kind of place at all, I would have said, yet this was where she headed. I let time pass. As I approached I saw her crying by the window.

Beautiful women are easier to follow, as a rule, because they expect to be watched. Men's eyes are sunlight on their skin. Being more confident, however, they are also more likely to challenge you if they feel that you've become assiduous. I was terribly embarrassed by my fortieth subject, Jessica C, or Jess. A brittle character, I think she rather enjoyed directing other women's attention towards how burdened she was with men's. *Why are you following me everywhere?* she said loudly as we queued for entry to the swimming pool. I looked curiously around to see who she might mean, so she repeated the question. The cashier and the mother with her children stopped what they were doing. *Me?* I said in the end, *I'm not.* But I'm no actor. In any case she was past soothing. I'd been in a couple of these scrapes before, so I understood that I had to leave. I was calm about it, outwardly, not like the first time. That involved a younger woman from a Lebanese family, Larissa A, my seventh subject. I was pretending to look at watches in a jeweller's window when she strode out and shouted simply, *Leave me alone!* On that occasion I protested my innocence for a long time. I couldn't let go, calling her paranoid and all that, and only walked away when a security guard was called.

Why does women's beauty so obsess them? Clearly their fertility fades faster than men's, meaning that a woman's sexual desirability is linked to how youthful she appears, and is thus scarcer and more valued. Yet arousing men's desire is hardly difficult, not for a woman of breeding age. Nor do they need to compete strenuously with one another for the lusts of the best men, since each man can have sex with hundreds of women and, knowing he need not be impeded by pregnancy or children, he might as well. Really you'd think a woman shouldn't focus her efforts on making men desire her, but on convincing one of them that she would make a good wife, thereby doubling the resources available to her children. To this end, beauty might actually be a hindrance, because when a man sees a beautiful young woman he knows that she will have more opportunities to be unfaithful to him if they marry. She may not take those opportunities, or she may. This is the man's challenge: to have as much sex as he can, naturally, but also to find one woman who will be faithful to him, for fear of unknowingly devoting his efforts to the care of another man's children. When he appraises a woman he must wonder whether sexual eagerness or a taste for subterfuge or risk-taking look like fixtures of her character.

I've come to presume that this is why women are so often obsessed with beauty, because it conveys clues to personality. If a woman conspicuously tries to make herself desirable then a man can guess that being desired matters more to her than average. This might or might not mean that she is in general very eager for sex, but it is unlikely to mean she is very reluctant. After all, why would any woman risk being thought lustful unless she was, given the harm that it will do her hopes of attracting a husband? This explains why female self-presentation has followed the path of ever greater naturalness since the food supply became secure. Looser hair, less structured clothes, less clothing in general: the desired effect is no longer a rich display of beauty but a display of how little work the beauty took, and women take great pains in order to achieve it. All that private striving for young-looking skin, firm-seeming breasts, temporarily shining hair and so on. No wonder they get paranoid.

I remember feeling frightened as I entered the Rose Cafe. I remember ordering the coffee and regretting it, my mouth already dry, my heart like a bad tyre at ninety. I didn't know what I was doing. I only knew that she was crying and I wanted to be with her, like the day before. I'd have no memory of what we said if I had not recorded it with a device in my pocket. The voice itself. Her sad and grateful voice.

I'm fine, it says.

Sorry, I know it's none of my business. Is there anything you need? Is there anyone I can call?

It's OK. I . . . It's OK.

I understand. Whatever it is, I'm sorry.

Thank you.

It's probably the last thing you want, some stranger trying to be nice. It just felt heartless to ignore you.

Don't worry. I'll be fine.

[She wants to be left alone but you can hear her smile.]

I didn't want to be, you know, the Bad Samaritan. Or whoever the person is at the beginning of that story. The one who walks past on the other side?

[A garland of her laughter. Hard to tell if she's amused by my gaucheness or likes my style. I don't know myself if I was trying to be funny. I just know her cheeks bunched like apricots. And something else. Something I'm only remembering now. It was hard to keep leaning over and I was careful to give her space, but I had to put my hand on the edge of her seat to support myself. I'd forgotten that. Throughout our meeting I gave her smooth leg the respectful distance she was entitled to expect. Some men would have brushed against her on purpose. I don't do that kind of thing.]

A high priest, I think, she says.

I'm not religious or anything. I just mean it felt wrong

that people might see you and no one would show they cared.

Well, thank you. I'm not religious either but I'll be fine. You're free from your dilemma.

[My laugh this time. I don't like my laugh.]

Oh believe me, I say. I've got more dilemmas where that came from. That doesn't mean you have to ask me about them.

[I sound like I'm straining a little. Maybe that's when I put my hand on her seat.]

Good. Thank you. And look, if you're curious. It's just a work thing, OK? Nobody died. I'm not dying. I don't get upset usually. It's just people being arseholes, you know. A hard couple of days but I'll be fine.

People are arseholes. Definitely. That's more or less a rule, I think. Everybody's decent inside, but we're all arseholes out here. We are sometimes anyway.

The guy I'm thinking of, my boss, he's an arsehole pretty much continuously.

[My laugh again. She says something but a blast of steam from the kitchen covers it. Something something *overconfident*, or *over on people*.]

When the steam stops I'm saying,

like a really bad one. I don't think I've met many as bad as that.

Lucky you.

Lucky me.

What do you do?

[She sips her tea. You can hear the suction as the cup approaches and the silence when it meets her lips.]

I'm a writer.

[This is what I always say to people. I've found it's a way to explain not having a job.]

What do you write?

[This is what people always ask.]

Oh lots of different stuff. Whatever comes along. I make a lot of notes.

Will I have read anything you've written?

No, no. I shouldn't think so.

I'm Frances by the way.

I tell her my name.

She feels that it's at least partly a show of attraction, and she partly doesn't mind. She'd rather be an object of lust than an object of pity, if that's the choice, although it is odd to be approached while crying, not exactly slick or tactful. The man seems nice, a bit klutzy and buffoonish, which might innocently explain his hobnailed timing. And it cheers her up. His embarrassment gives hers company. It's also interesting that he's a writer, interesting that that's his answer anyway. She gets the feeling it's more of a hobby, really. He's probably embarrassed about his real job. She knows how that goes.

Listen, she says. It's been nice meeting you. It really has. You've definitely been the Good Samaritan today, but I have to run.

OK. Sure. Of course.

He looks a bit deflated.

Sorry. You really have helped. I think I know now what I need to do.

Hey, no problem. I come here quite often so maybe I'll bump into you again.

Maybe. Absolutely. Look, here's my card. No, wait.

She crosses out the office number and scribbles her mobile in its place. When they shake hands to say goodbye it already seems too formal for them. They smile like they both know.

I've been re-reading Montaigne's *Essays* recently. Do you know them? Among those few of us with the means to spend our time considering how to spend our time, Montaigne gave my favourite answer: shut yourself up in a tower and write about the impossibility of the whole thing. He's been a comfort and an inspiration. I read the *Essays* and I think, *I'm not alone alone,* which itself justifies the writing, for me if not for him. In my most hopeful moments I imagine passing on the favour.

Montaigne claimed to rejoice in his appalling memory, saying it was the one thing he deserved to be famous for, and writers who edit as much as he did certainly have fame in mind. People with bad memories are less tempted to be dishonest, he says in 'On Liars', because they know that they'll have trouble keeping track of their fabrications. He elaborates the point with tales of cunning courtiers who eventually wind up in a dungeon or without a head. As so often with Montaigne the essay is marked as much by the messiness as by the originality of its thinking, and as so often this is its great joy, his preference for an honest muddle above false smoothness. For one thing, the lying courtiers he mentions might have carried off their intrigues if they'd just kept better records, a point he does not address. Indeed knowing they can't remember things reliably might make people more organised deceivers, whereas the good rememberers get overconfident and trip on their mistakes. I can only say might, and so should Montaigne, because of course it is impossible to know, by definition, how many liars succeed. Moreover I dispute his diagram of the knowing liar's mind in which the truth lingers hazardously at ankle height. The knowing liars that I've known, and known about, generally grow so accustomed to their invented version of events that it overwrites their memory of what happened. Some I think even knowingly rely on this to comb the knots out of their conscience and thus make them better liars. None of us can know, by definition again, whether we've convinced ourselves of falsehoods in this way, but I think most of us realise that there exists a mechanism by which repetition hardens into instinct. Think, say, of how true reading or driving only emerge once you're unconscious of them. I actually type faster without any awareness of the keys.

An inconvenient result of this is that you often can't make the distinction that Montaigne does between the innocence and the knowingness in our behaviour, although you can see why Montaigne would want the distinction made. As he says, he has hurt the feelings of many friends down the years by forgetting promises and favours. *They bring my affections into question upon the account of my memory, and from a natural imperfection make out a defect of conscience,* he protests as if it were impossible for him – a man surrounded by servants and obsessed with writing things down – to arrange to be reminded of anything worth the trouble. Knowing that he was indeed letting down his friends, and perhaps feeling bad about it, he had good reason to wish fame on the *merveilleuse défaillance* of his *mémoire* and thus remove the conscious part of himself from guilt. Indeed I fancy that Montaigne began as just the kind of conscious liar that he advocates pursuing with fire and the sword, before graduating to the unconscious kind who truly believes he has the authority to make such advocations. He lied about loving his friends, then about his memory being to blame, then repeated both lies so often that he thought they were true. This makes him little different from the rest of us. We live instinctively, for the most part, and afterwards decorate the behaviour with rationales. Knowingly or unknowingly, Montaigne may even have invited this reading of 'On Liars'. It is certainly a true picture of the liar that he was.

This stuff matters to me. I can't help it. I want to explain what happened and answer questions, yours and mine. I want to understand the choices that have marooned me here and it makes me a student of the journey. Did entering her house mean that I was bound to end up talking to Frances in that cafe? Did interfering with my subjects' lives mean that I was bound to end up trapped in her house? Did following Laura mean that I was bound to end up interfering? Or is this just me? Was I bound to end up doing all of this, things being what they were, me being who I am? Have I travelled down a slope, off a cliff edge, or by my own effort along flat ground? I can only consult my memory in search of answers, and like Montaigne write everything down, though I know that as well as a machine for writing I am one for remembering conveniently. This is how we survive, by getting used to things. Time drags us from our wreckage.

I knew I would have to study Frances from a greater distance after meeting her, and perhaps less frequently, or with radical and reluctant countermeasures like a disguise. I thought about this carefully on the way home, still a professional, giving due diligence to the paths I wouldn't take. That's if I remember rightly. Perhaps I'd already decided everything and wanted the appearance of deliberation. Sometimes you don't want to know what's next.

SHE IS HEAVY WITH SLEEP. Sleep clogs her skin. She reaches out for water but must have finished it in the night because her glass is all light and empty and only a trickle makes her tongue. She's heard that people sleep in waves or cycles so perhaps she's swum up suddenly from sleep's depths. Strange on a day with no alarm.

She slops downstairs and clears herself an area among the debris, makes tea, and eats. Toast helps her head but not her stomach. Outside another bright morning has been arranged. Quarrelly blackbirds, mooing collared doves, all that. Clouds cast and uncast panes of sun on her plate. Gilded and dulled crumbs, gilded and dulled. Nowhere to go today.

The one good email on her phone comes from James, a lawyer and briefly a boyfriend. He has enclosed the letter he proposes to send to Jenny, the director of legal services, the executive chairman, and Will. *On behalf of my client . . . remind you of your responsibility under . . . seek redress using all legal means as described . . .* It is too much for her. She taps out her approval and thanks and returns to bed.

Awake again, better, she puts on sturdy underwear, leggings and a T-shirt with more past than future. Her hair she ties back in a ponytail before seeking out the running shoes like forgiven friends. The day's gone flat and cold but she is soon warm again, breath rhythmical. The road bends east. Where it begins to scoop uphill she wades against it hard, proud and impervious, lost in her machine. She's running. She is running. She is winning. She is winning the war on mass.

She'll turn back at that tree. That is the decision. She'll get there and she'll run home. And again tomorrow. And again. Her head and arms flap, tiring. She hasn't the strength to keep her strides long during the descent and her feet stamp their landings. Her mouth's gone gluey. Were she a spitter she would spit. On. On home through the rain's first whisperings.

Morning! Been running?

Steph is reading her phone with a mug of tea. There are now two plates of toast crumbs on the table.

Yes.

Frances breathes.

I have.

Good for you.

I could. Have gone longer but. I thought it better just to. Build up gradually. I haven't run much recently I. Haven't had time.

Yeah, yeah, yeah. It's so important to make a habit of it. That's why I joined the gym. You know the money's coming out of your bank account and that keeps you going. I really recommend it. The treadmills are sprung, which is much better for your joints, and they've got TVs to watch. Otherwise it gets so boring, you know? And you can have a sauna afterwards. I really enjoy it these days.

Steph's rather eagerly grasped the role of adviser now that Frances is the one whose life is going wrong, now that Frances is the straggler. Besides, this isn't why she joined the gym. She joined because Greg chivvied her with regular light-hearted remarks about her shape, and paid. They discussed it all about six months ago. Obviously there's a deal now that the discussion is forgotten.

You're right. I keep meaning. To get around to it.

She takes an apple, and is in the bathroom when Steph yells.

What?

There was a phone call for you!

Who was it?

Jeremy Hafford? Is that right?

Hapgood. Shit, you mean Jeremy Hapgood?

The executive chairman. She leans out across the bannisters, a towel around her.

That's it.

You mean his PA called?

No, he did. He was very nice. He wanted to know if you could go in to have a chat with him today. It sounded important.

Shit. Yes, I bet it did. He's the boss of the whole company,

Steph. I was telling you about him last night.

Very plummy?

Yes. Jesus. What did he say?

He's the actual boss?

The thought of Stephanie, half-dressed, hungover, the phone in her hand, her toast in the other, Hapgood on the line . . .

Yes. What did he say?

Oh, well, just that really. He said he wanted to have a chat with you, and when I said you were out he left a number.

How did he sound? Was he tense? Annoyed?

No, I wouldn't say he was annoyed.

What *would* you say? Jesus, Steph!

Oh, quite cheerful really. Quite relaxed.

And it is true. Frances finds a voicemail message. Hapgood sounds genial and calm, almost doting. He asks if she'd have time to visit him today to talk about *all this*.

She is taking her best suit to the cleaners. She couldn't see much wrong with it herself but Steph carried it out into the daylight, gave it backhand scuffs to the lapels and pronounced it failed. They were on the point of disagreeing, when a man arrived with pizza. They hadn't ordered pizza. That's what they told him, and he didn't take it at all well, but his struggle to be rude to them in a second language made them laugh and afterwards Frances relented. The dry cleaner says that the Executive Express service guarantees the suit's return within two hours. He says it again when she explains it is important, she has a meeting at five. He has a young face and tired eyes, but she only sees his mighty beard and the knitted kufi on his head. They reassure her. You expect a fundamentalist to be prompt.

When she collects the suit she can see that Stephanie was right. It looks beautiful. But dressing makes her nervous. It's hard to look impressive without picking up the mindset of impressing. She arrives at work in good time, if it is still work, and is glad to see the other security guard on duty today. She has no swipe card and doesn't want to alert Hapgood to her earliness by calling up from the front desk, so she sits on a green sofa pretending to read the choice of newspapers in several languages. At 4.48 she checks the clock, then at 4.50, then 4.53. At 4.55 she approaches the desk. They were expecting her and have no need to call upstairs. They point to the feared lift. Up on Hapgood's floor his PA proffers a seat on a blue sofa. Sometimes they do pitches in the meeting rooms up here, and afterwards march back down with their opinions. Frances puts her phone on silent and stares at the doors a while. She wonders whether Hapgood remembers the afternoon subgroup at the summer conference where they'd unleashed their creativity designing stickers. She expects he's a secretly good rememberer.

At 5.06 Hapgood breaks through the doors to greet her so cordially, and so close, that she can't stand up until he's finished.

Thank you so much for coming in at such short notice, he says, continuing to shake her hand despite the strangeness of the angle. It's such a horrid situation and I always feel the best thing is to talk in person.

He will be about sixty. He has the becoming plumpness of the lifestage. Arms spread wide and waistcoat showing, he goes star-shaped like a teddy.

I agree, she says, to show she has her own experiences. She's not been summoned. That isn't what this is.

Will, spindly, quite another species, is already in the office. And poor Jenny again, standing apart from the three chairs at the nearside of Hapgood's beefy desk. Will weaves over to Frances palms up, head slanted, as though they are such incorrigible old pals the two of them, they really are, to fight like this. Fleetingly it looks like he wants a hug.

Would you like a coffee? Tea? The pot is fresh.

This is Hapgood. Sunset glows behind him.

No, thank you.

William? Jenny?

Both shake their heads.

Very well then. Shall we discuss this?

He looks at Will and Frances, two looks of equal length, and takes his seat. They sit after him.

First of all, and most importantly of all, I want to say how sorry I am for what you're going through, Frances. Truly. The email must have been a nasty shock, and now it's been followed by this suspension. If you feel let down – and Will said you were very disappointed – then I understand. Indeed I'd expect it. I hope we've not given the impression somehow that you should feel differently. I also think it's quite right that you've been talking to your lawyer. This letter, he waves at his computer, seems sensible. What I want to do, if you'll permit me, is explain the board's position to you in more detail, and fill in some of the blanks about why we decided as we did. I should have done it sooner, actually. I'm sorry about that too.

Frances says it's OK.

Thank you. That's very gracious. The board's position is essentially this: we think the allegations against you are serious, but we can't see any evidence to support them. We all think that you are innocent therefore, and are eager to prove it. When we discussed the matter during a long meeting yesterday morning it became clear that we had three options: to dismiss the email out of hand as an obvious smear; to ask you some questions and look into the matter casually; or finally, the option we have chosen, to investigate the whole affair as thoroughly as possible, which necessitates your being briefly suspended. Having talked it over, I think we all felt that this was the only way to exonerate you properly. The horrible thing about this sort of situation, as I'm sure you've felt yourself, is the no-smoke-without-fire mentality that can take hold. Unfortunately people enjoy repeating rumours, even without evidence. From your point of view, that threatens to darken a very promising career. And it makes you less able to do your job effectively, from ours. We are a consulting firm. Good people are really our only asset, as you know, so your future here is not a trivial matter. Those few staff who know about this email have been asked not to discuss it until we are able to show them evidence to verify or disprove its allegations. And I believe those people have agreed?

Will nods.

I understand, Frances, that you do not believe that the

board is acting in your interests, or you may see your interests differently, so the only thing I want to convince you of today is our belief, the board's unanimous belief, that suspending you is the best way to protect a valuable asset of this company, which is what you are.

Frances knows she is here to be charmed. Angrily she feels it working.

It's true, honestly, Will says. The last thing any of us wanted was to alienate you. Which means, he ventures laughter, that we obviously didn't do a brilliant job.

Hapgood laughs with him. Frances gives a wary smile.

Jenny's not given us a very flattering report, have you, Jenny? Hapgood calls across the room.

So how long do I have to wait? Frances asks.

Hapgood's seat squeaks as he reclines to ponder this.

I want to give you an answer, he says at last. You deserve one. But the truth is I don't know. Obviously we're desperate to get all this behind us as soon as possible, and to get you back in the office. I have stressed this to the people handling the investigation. I'm told we'll have a clearer view of how long everything will take within a day or two, although obviously it has to be accurate and thorough.

I agree. But that's what worries me, if I may say so. I have done nothing wrong. I know that. I also know that someone out there is trying to damage my reputation. You say that's what the board assumes too? That this is a malicious rumour, as you put it?

Absolutely. But we need proof.

In that case how do you know, how do I know, that people won't lie to your investigators? Or spread more lies for them to find? Will I be consulted? What if it's my word against theirs?

You're right. These are important questions, and it is frustrating. All I can say is that you are presumed innocent by everybody here. The purpose of looking into this so thoroughly is to find out the truth and not be swayed by rumours. The board will decide afterwards what to do.

Suspending me looks like a presumption of guilt, don't you think?

Not at all. We work in areas of intense commercial sensitivity, as you know. This is just best practice.

The reason for your suspension, Will joins in, is so that you can come back with a clean slate. If you were in the office, we'd need to keep you away from possible evidence, which means it would be impractical for you to continue your work as normal, and we'd have to explain that. We'd also run the risk of people one day saying you had influenced the outcome. This way, we can just tell anyone who asks that you're working on a new pitch at home, or visiting a potential client whose details we can't reveal. So far no one has asked, fortunately.

I thought you were against it, Will?

I'm against how it must feel for you. I was worried about that. And I certainly didn't relish telling you. As I've said, I probably didn't do it very well. But I suppose I can now see the wisdom of what Jeremy's saying.

How about the person who falsely accused me? They haven't been suspended. Why can't they influence the outcome of this?

Hapgood takes this one.

We don't know who they are, of course. And I gather it seems likely that they are not an employee of this company.

Will I be asked what I think?

Of course. Do you have any ideas? William says you told him you were stumped.

She knows it's not advisable to take big decisions quickly during times of stress.

I do have some ideas, yes. I don't want to damage anybody's reputation by speaking without evidence, however.

That does you credit.

There is an interval. An interval or an impasse.

What I want, she says, is to know how long this is going to take, to be guaranteed my chance to see everything that you uncover, and to be able to defend myself – if necessary – to the board.

That all sounds reasonable, Will says. We'll discuss it and get back to you. The problem is that we can't make promises on behalf of the company without a board meeting. It's part of our legal responsibility to the other directors.

And a bloody nuisance, Hapgood adds.

Indeed. Hopefully in a couple of days we'll be able to offer something more concrete. Until then I know it's asking a lot, but you need to trust us.

A little scoff escapes from Frances.

Hapgood again,

I really am sorry. None of us wants to be in this situation, and it's far worse for you than for anybody else. I realise that. But if you are prepared to wait, you will accumulate a lot of gratitude. I don't know, and this isn't a promise, but I expect it won't be more than three weeks before this is all behind us.

Three *weeks*?

She is round-eyed. She had not considered this.

Perhaps less. Although in the scheme of things that isn't long. Sorry, I don't know. Jenny, can you help?

We just don't know. I'm sorry, Jeremy.

Seriously? Three weeks?

This is why I shouldn't speculate. I'm sorry, Frances. You'll be on full pay of course for the duration, however long it is. And we'll be in touch the moment we have news.

He seems to be tiring of her, or of the day. She wonders whether this meeting was Will's idea or his.

It's a really tough one, Will says.

And something breaks.

OK, she says. I'll tell you my thoughts. I don't know if he mentioned it, but I found out that Will was in the QTel building at the time the email was sent. Did he mention that?

Hapgood looks at his hand.

I think whoever investigates this needs to ask Will why he was there, and talk to QTel staff to ascertain the exact times that he was with them, when he was logged into the network, and so on. They should also look at his role in bringing this matter to your attention, and his comments to the board. If I'm suspended, he should be suspended too. Couldn't falsely accusing someone of a crime also result in criminal proceedings? Jenny?

I'm sorry. I don't know. I will look into it.

Will is calm.

Frances, he says. I told you and the board why I was there.

Me and hundreds of others, I should think.

And how many of those others feel threatened by me?

I don't know how to answer that, except to say that I don't. You're a valuable part of the team, an essential part, the very opposite of a threat to anybody. I've loved working with you. I know you've had a rough time, so this kind of reaction is understandable, but it really is just lashing out.

Let's not prejudge the investigation, Will.

Hapgood stands up.

Right then. I think we've accomplished all we're going to today.

She is drinking alone, having taken herself out into the night-time, into the changed world. It's not something she can recall doing before, going spontaneously into a pub to drink like this, although to be fair the decision wasn't really a spontaneous thing, more what she was left with after the hands had been grimly shaken and she was alone in the silence of the lift and the thoughts began to swarm. She could not just sit on a train like this was nothing. She couldn't take a taxi home. The thoughts would riot. Even on the street they coiled feverishly, looking for purchase in her mouth or ears, slithering up her nose. So she's come here, to the Rising Sun, to hide in hubbub and to drink, and when Stephanie calls she turns off her phone. She and Will can no longer work together, not now, so without grounds for a termination the company will have to move her to another team or another office. It will be made to look like a promotion. She'll be given what she'll be told is an important job to do, but it'll be thankless and she'll hate it, and now and then she'll get a tour of what she's lost. She'll be overworked or underworked into a state of abject pliancy. The disgruntled you quarantine and do not give the relief of a quick cull. Seeing this path ahead, the board may even ditch the investigation and bring her back. Let the rumours do their work. She won't know what's been said, or is being said, or if anything is. These thoughts will be ineradicable. It'll be a comfort at first to be told she's paranoid, then a diagnosis. Should she get ready to fight? Does she want victory? Maybe better a planned swim to the next boat through flat water. Maybe. Maybe. She needs time. Right now it's difficult to hear anything above the screeching of *Ruin Will! Ruin Will! Ruin Will!*

Excuse me. Listen, I know it's rude and cheesy and everything. You probably just want to be left alone. But I've noticed you've been sat there for ages like you're totally lost in thought. And I can't help myself. I'm dying to know what it's all about.

A man has stepped from the crowd. This again. Twice in two days.

Dying to? Frances says.

Well . . . I mean, you look worried. Unless you're waiting for someone?

He smiles. He has the slovenly hang of a guy who has reluctantly accepted the obviousness of his good looks. He is also tall, and muscular like nobody in offices. He has that beard that's popular right now, and which Frances isn't keen on as a rule, but which she admits suits him. The man is gorgeous, as a matter of fact. He'll be something like a plumber, probably, just paid. She knows such men from hiring them, the self-employed knights errant of the cities who, when young, work twelve-hour days and live in cash and are blushingly heroised by the incapable. They con you a little, just for pride. The whistling nihilists. She likes them.

No, she says.

Does that mean you'll tell me?

I'll tell you. It's dull, but if you're *dying to know* I'll tell you.

I am. I'm Patrick. Can I get you another drink? It's the least I can do.

He is pointing to her glass. She nods. *This is a pick-up,* say his eyes. *I'm not pretending this is not a pick-up. I'm not pretending you don't realise this is a pick-up. Nobody's pretending anything. I'm going to try to pick you up.*

She tells him everything, and he listens, nodding speciously. It's loud and they lean close. Covering what her job involves, who her colleagues are, their competing interests, it all takes time, but Patrick is patient, and must be listening because he neglects his beer. He's not a plumber. She discovers that. He owns his own delivery company, he says, and she sees him enjoy saying it. When they at last get to her suspension, he is volcanic.

They've *suspended* you? You're joking?

No.

They can't do that.

Of course they can. They have. It might not be legal, but they've done it. Am I going to force my way into the office every day?

That's a fucking disgrace. Excuse my language.

Yes. It is.

Outrageous!

I know.

She spots glints of parody in his partisanship. He seems to be overplaying the sympathy in a deliberate yet deniable way, almost mocking her problems, which she almost likes. Better than pretending sympathy is what he's mainly feeling. He is mocking the whole men and women thing, women and men, all the coy procedures. She likes this a great deal. It isn't knowing you're going to fuck that's sexy. It's knowing that you both know. It's ulteriority. It's being in secret already intertwined.

You need a lawyer.

I have a lawyer.

Is he any good?

We'll find out.

The idea of Patrick as a connoisseur of lawyers makes her smile.

Another? He is pointing to her glass again.

Is it possible, she wonders, for each of them to believe that they are using the other and for them each to be correct? Or is that just what the used believe? Can whole relationships be built on mutual using? Are any built otherwise?

Sure, she says. But I'll get these. What are you having?

She is unexpectedly drunk. Enjoying it. Three quick big gins and life's a colourful inconsequence. *Fuck it,* they make her brain say. Fuck work, fuck life, fuck all her doubts about this man, all breath and antlers. His hard flanks. Fuck while the thoughts are sleeping.

She sways in for service at the bar. A roar of workmates from other workplaces, hip-deep in an unbuttoning of the day. She and her own colleagues do this sometimes, but never here. Too close to the office. She glances over the road and sees people she knows, actually, lined up behind the door. One of them is Will. He splits from the group and approaches the kerb. When the traffic splits he opens up a jog. A car might come. No lights by some drunk's oversight. It might crash his leg bones. He crosses safely. He is going to the station. She is pushing through the crowd. Through the tables even. On to the street.

Will! she bellows.

He turns.

Will!

She is advancing.

Two things, really, Will. Firstly, I know what you're doing, you fucking arsehole. And secondly, fuck you.

He just laughs.

Frances, he manages. Have you had a drink or two?

I know, Will. Just understand that. Keep playing your bullshit games, but remember I am watching. And I am going to sue.

Listen, Frances . . .

No, no, Will. You listen. I'm watching. Remember that. I'm watching you.

I'll make a note of it. Watching me. OK.

He walks away.

You do that.

People are looking.

You do that, Will!

BEFORE BED I PREPARED THE VAN. Stakeouts go wrong if you're not serious about them. I know from experience. Some neighbour comes knuckling on the window. *Can I ask what you're doing here?* God help you if they see a camera. Some years ago therefore, I rigged up a system, which I have since refined. It is easy to assemble if you apply yourself and it is necessary, be assured. I've survived enough scrapes to know that you'd not be wise to rely on luck.

You'll need a large car with foldable back seats or, if you have the means, you'll buy a van as I did. Get a laptop with a spare battery and the smallest external webcam you can find. Miniature ones are available from surveillance shops, or you may be able to shrink a conventional model by removing the casing. The camera needs attaching somewhere discreet with a view through a window. I dug mine into the padding of the passenger's and driver's headrests. Remember you'll need to tilt the lens as required by where you park, and run the cable to the laptop in the back. No doubt wireless models are now available, but I just tape the cable down the side of the seat. If you're using a car, you'll need to load it with a large hollow item such as a wardrobe, in which you and your computer will hide. Be realistic about comfort, though. You may need to stay there for a long time. You'll see the advantage of a van.

When I arrived it was not quite dawn. Having parked in the best spot I could find, I climbed into the complete black of the van's interior, my stomach tightening. More than six hours I would sit in just the light of the screen. I recorded everything, but I'd had to park quite far down, and as a result only the top of her door was visible above a hedge. To catch it opening I'd need to be attentive. On the other hand, the camera's slanted aspect put a good length of pavement into view, so if I did miss Frances leaving I'd have perhaps half a minute to see her walking along the road, if she did not cross it. At nine the commuters had come and gone without sight of her. It crossed my mind that she had slept elsewhere.

Suddenly she ran out in sports clothes and disappeared. It happened so fast that I felt lucky to have seen her, although I didn't know what to make of it at first. Was she running somewhere? Or just running? I had guessed the latter, given how she was dressed, but it was an anxious wait for her return. When she did return, reddened, after twenty-one minutes, she rested momentarily with her hands on her thighs before letting herself in. Evidently she wasn't at work today, or at least this morning. A shower would follow, I presumed, so I set upon my sandwiches and coffee. I can never wait until lunchtime for a packed lunch.

At eleven I was irritable. I was mostly angry with myself because in spite of the coffee I'd passed through one of those grim somnolent spells. You know, when the head droops, rebounds, begins to droop again, and stuck in the van I could do little to prevent it. I found a restful nook above the wheel arch, and there awoke sharply, knowing I might have missed her. I hadn't been asleep for long, but the recording revealed nothing helpful. Vehicles often stopped or slowed to let each other pass, blocking my view, and there'd been a few of these while I was sleeping. The whole thing left me tetchily irresolute. I did want to know why she was not at work, but for how long should I keep waiting? Increasingly it seemed likely that I would leave with nothing accomplished, and knowing that I might have left a minute too soon.

So I ordered pizza. This is the kind of impatient gesture I have warned you about, I know, but I am not a perfect implementer of my principles. I hope I am at least honest about that. From past experiences, I knew that pizza generally prods some life out of a house, and indeed the door did open. I saw some curly hair, presumably Stephanie's, bobbing just above the hedge. Soon afterwards, Stephanie left. With a better angle I might have seen her double-lock the door, or call goodbye to somebody inside. I resolved to wait an hour more, and about half had passed when Frances appeared, carrying a hanger of clothes towards the shops.

My back ached, and outside the van the light was nearly blinding, but I limped quickly across the road with my bag, rang the bell and waited. No one appeared, so I took the keys out of my pocket. I'd made perhaps a dozen attempts at home the night before, and brought what I thought were the three best. Blanks and cutting machines are easy to find, but working self-taught from only putty impressions involves an amount of grinding, peering, filing, bleeding, swearing and the like that leaves little feeling of success. By the end I was trying less in the belief that one of the keys would work, more in order to prove to myself that when I failed there would be no need to try again. In some ways I actually hoped to feel all three stick in the tumblers, their intransigence in spite of my coaxing meaning I was honourably spared. However, the mechanism unlatched easily, not quite on the first go but soon after. Success seemed to leave no choice. I had to make my installations.

—

Naturally in the early days, once I felt settled in my studies, my thoughts turned away from theoretical anxieties and ever more towards technique. Chiefly I began to presume that bugs, webcams, homing beacons and surveillance devices generally would become my daily tools, so I acquired many of them, and familiarised myself eagerly, having always enjoyed the process of acquaintanceship with new technology. Successes were rare, however, and in the end I had to admit my disappointment. The problem was not that the devices failed, though there were those times. They were also incriminating and traceable if found, but that was not the problem either. The problem, really, was that they worked too well.

At this stage, you have to understand, I wasn't good at this. Without comparators, I don't know if I'm good at it now, but back then I was worse, for sure. I lost people, frequently, and this primed me to believe that information was scarce and precious, that I could never have too much. I first understood the mistakenness of this way of thinking with subject eighteen, Nina M, who was a script writer and editor, though it was hard to say how successfully she was either, and indeed trying to say became my point of interest. Nina worked most days in a coffee shop near her home. The place was large, and did little business outside mealtimes. Presumably for this reason management did not seem to mind Nina and a number of other regulars lingering all day, ordering little, sometimes even making phone calls in their seats. I was lucky because a laundrette stood across the road, where I could easily watch while washing. Despite not hearing any of the conversations between the regulars, I gradually formed the view that it was insensitive, this state of residence, since it transformed the cafe from one workplace into two, and as a result made the work of the table staff a kind of servitude. The discomfort I felt watching, and the sullenness that I fancied I saw in the servers' eyes, did not derive *per se* from their poor pay in relation to the freelancers they served, nor because of any high-handedness I saw on the freelancers' part, but rather because of the collegial spirit that existed around them but without them. Normally servers have this to themselves, and it gives them the dignity of hosting customers on their own turf, but the freelancers took this away by memorising the menus and knowing the table numbers and asking after the cook by name. (And he, Alfredo, did not help things by so often coming out to greet them.) At first I held Nina guilty only of thoughtlessness. Later I began to believe that she did enjoy her dominion over the table staff because it balanced her own feelings of professional inadequacy. If she knew she was not yet admired for her work, she could at least be resented. Far from being insensitive, it was sensitivity malignly applied.

Anyway, the difficulty of the situation for me was that I could not spend time there without myself becoming one of the regulars. I knew that Nina had her own table opposite the door, table four, so late one afternoon, when she had left, I went and sat there and affixed a tiny transmitting microphone with a wad of chewing gum to the table's underside. The signal from this microphone I could receive and record across the road with another device inside my washing. I bought a dozen table cloths, and various uniforms and napkins, and got a story ready about being a contract caterer. I began to feel that this was not enough to explain my staying in the laundrette for days on end, however, so I installed a different microphone, one which would store recordings rather than transmit them. It was slightly larger, but still easy to bury in the gum. After four days in total, I gave up. The bugging wasn't difficult. What was, which I had not considered, was managing all of the material that bugging makes. The microphone was noise-activated of course, but in a coffee shop, and indeed in most public places, there is always noise, which ends up creating maybe five hours of tape each day. Once you've been over the hard to hear sections several times, that's at least eight of listening. I could fairly quickly find Nina's arrival in the morning. She'd be greeted by the other regulars or by the staff, be asked how she was, and give a brief description. The rest was an ordeal. I don't know about you, but I can't concentrate for long on the sound of nothing happening. The lunch choices of other customers, their conversations with their wives and boyfriends and clients, even Nina's conversations with them, and her chats about friends' love lives, the clatter of crockery and the endless, endless shrieks of the coffee machine . . . There may well have been some good material there, but I wouldn't know because I spent most of the time in a stupor, too bored to hear it. I'd formulate the next day's plans, or think about past subjects, and the tape would run on and on. Then I'd notice, reprove myself, rewind, and start losing interest again. I began to resent Nina myself, for putting me through it.

Since Nina I've understood that technology has particular uses. I'll use it to record a moment that I expect to be interesting, or when I need to follow someone in real time in order to react, such as with that young mother in the service station. Otherwise it's a last resort, like my wallet plan for Amelia. I explain this now in order to give context to my sense of wonder at what I got from Frances. In a way I was breaking my own rules by installing the equipment speculatively, but I did expect the house to be quiet, and I felt that it would help me stay out of sight, having so impulsively introduced myself to her the previous day. Plus it was an opportunity I'd not had before and might never have again.

I tried to walk casually back to the van. As far as I could tell the devices were working properly, though it was hard to say for sure in a silent house. Moments later she returned, no longer carrying the clothes. My breathing became loud in my headphones like I was the whole world.

She shut the door. I heard it. Thenceforth I heard all the other little shifts and whispers of her behaviour. Oh, but it was glorious! I'm not sure I've ever known such free-wheeling rapture. The whooshing of her steam iron and the way the stand rattled when she put it down. The clinks of tea-making. Her singing with the radio on. Such unprotectedness. Yet there I was, protecting her.

Presently Stephanie returned and I got all their talk. Stephanie had a boyfriend but Frances didn't. They discussed the forthcoming meeting, and the shape of her predicament. How I pined to comfort her. I wanted to be with her all the time. When she left I could have walked up to her and taken her hand without a word.

But I let her go. I knew where she was going, and that I had to be there. In triumph, I drove home. I put music on myself and sang. On my return I showered, ate, backed up all the data, and excitedly made notes still in a towel. When the time came to leave, I had to force myself to stop writing.

I should quickly explain my policy on disguises. I think the trick, insofar as there is a trick, is not to try to look like someone else, as anything below mastery only draws the eye. Instead I dress as an aspect or a version of myself. Studies suggest that hair is recognition's reference point, so I slick mine back, and add to this plain-lensed spectacles. This changes how I look enough, I think, to deflect most glances. Those who stare may recognise me, it is true, but I'll have nothing but my style choices to account for. Consider by contrast how you might explain a false moustache or nose. In short the aim is not to conceal yourself entirely. It is to conceal that anything is being concealed.

Dressed thus therefore I taxied to the Rising Sun and I wasn't kept waiting. At 5.38 Frances drifted out of the building and across the street. All the way across and into the Rising Sun itself. *Steady*, I thought, gripping my drink. *Be steady here.* I'd sat in overlooking pubs so many times that I'd taken their safety almost as a rule. In their leisure time people like to be some distance from their work. I also knew to keep calm. A busy pub is a good hiding place.

She took a table far from me and drank a gin and tonic. I was at the front, where the best view of her office was, and it was difficult to look round. When I did look I saw she was alone and pale. I'd expected her to go directly to the station. I'd been half out of my seat to go with her. This silent drinking though, I didn't like it. It wasn't good at all. *Steady*. The thought was in my mind to lose the spectacles, ruffle my hair and stride into the picture. I was desperate to know what had happened, of course, but now I yearned even more to offer the comfort that only I could give. I also knew two days in a row would be strange.

I'd seen the man looking. I've become an expert in men's looks. He started talking. I don't know what he said and I didn't need to know. This shirted bulge, this dead anatomy. You know what his words are, and that he practises their use. You know he'd seen that she was prone. You see him smile at the right times and buy more drinks. (You watch sharply for adulterants.) He lets her do the talking, and you watch him nod, the ladies' man. You move round your table to get a better angle. You know they're talking about her work and see him feast on it indifferently. *Will.* She talks a lot about Will. Her boss, *that scumbag* you'd heard her say at home. The man grins like it's a big joke when what's funny is what'll happen to *him*. Men like him, men like Will. For them Frances is meat or money. Frances, the most precious of all. They know nothing about her. Who she really is. They have no place in her mind.

Frances went to the bar. She put her back against it while she waited. I turned to face the window in order not to be seen, though she had seemed to be gazing past me at her office. A man was leaving, the tall man I had seen escort her out the day before. Will himself, it had to be, with his jealousy and his sandwich ploy. Frances had told me all about his ways to keep her down. When I turned back to read her expression she had gone. Will flashed past my window. The ladies' man was staring at the door.

Will.

I heard her shout.

Will!

I couldn't get the rest cleanly, but it was like something left her with the shouting, because when she came back she looked abruptly smaller. The ladies' man got drinks and put a hand on her back which stayed there.

I stood and tried to leave without being seen.

Hi, Frances said.

Oh. Hi, I said. I was going to call. Are you OK?

Not really.

I'm Patrick.

An arm steamed in. I shook its hand.

I work just round the corner, I said like I needed to explain.

Oh yes? What business are you in?

He's a writer.

She remembered.

Yeah? What do you write about?

Oh anything really. Ideas, stories, stuff . . . Basically I just like writing and reading.

My company, we had a job with a publisher the other day. Matinee Press they were called. Do you know them?

I don't. I'm really sorry. I'm in a hurry. Good to meet you, Patrick. Frances, I'll call soon.

OK. I'll . . .

Whatever else she said I didn't catch.

Stations are crowded places, which tends to make you worry you will lose your subject if you don't keep close. This in turn can make you conspicuous and shifty. With experience, however, you learn that the opposite is true, that railway stations induce highly regular behaviour, meaning that if you do lose sight of someone you have an unusually good chance of finding them again, if you stay calm. There's usually only a short list of places they could go, remember and, when there, they usually wait. If they're running it will be to catch a train, which can be your reason to run after them. If they vanish search each platform, beginning with your best guess. Nothing is guaranteed of course, but you'll need bad luck to lose them altogether.

On this occasion it helped that refurbishment work had hidden the downward escalator and a section of the concourse behind blue hoardings. These funnelled the crowd and slowed Will down. I saw his head waiting to start the stairs, then at the bottom I saw which way he turned. When I arrived on the platform he was reading a large poster across the tracks, at the end where the trains scream in. It was an old advertisement, for coffee. The edges were peeling and torn. The whole wall behind us was untiled render. Above, where the electronic display and the security cameras ought to be, just the cables hung knotted and waiting. All along the platform it was the same. No cameras. No information. I jostled forwards until I was directly behind him. He'd finished with the coffee advert now, and put in earphones. He had his phone in both hands and was reading, like this was the most ordinary evening in the world.

The rails began to shiver and gleam. I doubt he noticed. I'm not sure he ever noticed anything. Some shuffling behind packed us tighter together. As the train approached I got a chestful of his elbows. He made no effort to withdraw them. The train roared. The noise was dizzying. I slipped a foot between his legs, wrapped my heel around his ankle and looking absently along the platform with my hand wedged in the shadows gave him a sharp push in the lower back. As he stumbled I grimaced and jerked my foot away as though trodden on. As he fell I reached out but failed to catch him. I did try. Because in fact I was a little early. He had a few seconds just draped on the rails. I'd not planned this, so I'd not worked on timings. It's the surprised eyes that I remember, and the grime on his suit. The glow of his phone on the blackened ground.

And though the driver was really quite prompt in putting the brakes on, we were at the fast end, as I say, so there was no chance at all to stop in time. There was just a swirling in the crowd, a kind of blunted surge, and someone shouting *Help him! Help him!* and Will shouting something inaudible, like there was anything that could be done. And in his struggles I think he must have touched the live rail because there was a heavy bang and that scared everybody back. There was a scattering of screams. He looked surprised at nothing now. He twitched a bit. I don't know the effects of electrocution on the body. I'm not a doctor. And he was lying slanted so one wheel, the near wheel, caught his trousers first and sort of wound them in, dragging the whole leg-half of his body inwards and tightening the cloth around the shin bone until the metal bit and one leg then the other sort of stiffened upwards and puckered off, the first leg more cleanly because of the inclusion of the ankle with the second, leaving only a partly crushed wet shoe to drop from the wheel's side. And during this there was a kind of gargle from him, but briefly, because the far wheel met his head straight afterwards, hair first then eye. It severed his earphone cable and kind of folded his skull contents through his mouth. And I don't know how much blood I had expected, I hadn't done any expecting, but there was a lot, though it didn't look like blood, it looked like oil, black oil, except when electric flashes lit the red. And there was smoke, but not the plastic-smelling kind machines make, something more natural. And crying. Someone fully wailing now. And the smack of perhaps a pint of something landing on the floor and the smell of vomit definitely. And the station manager and staff were fairly quick, to give them credit. Someone climbed in and reversed the train, and the others evacuated everyone except those of us who had been nearby and had seen the incident and were needed to give statements. We were led up the escalator to an office where we watched a pair of paramedics rushing down the stairs to do, we knew, no good at all.

We waited. We were told the police would come. And there were fourteen of us. We counted. A young couple, four commuters, an old lady, and a family of six tourists, I think. They spoke another language to each other. One of them, a boy about fourteen, had been the vomiter who we all felt sorry for and disgusted by. We waited until the authorities had found an interpreter and a fresh T-shirt for the boy and finally one of the commuters said, *Did anyone see what happened? Did he just trip?* And a few others said, *I think so.* And I said, *I was right behind him. I don't know what happened. I think he tried to step back. Maybe he got tangled with the woman next to me, but he trod on my foot. By the time I realised he was already falling. It was all so quick.* And the first person said, *Yes, he seemed to stumble on the way down.* There was an agreeing murmur and some mentions of his shoelaces, which might have been untied. People said the shoelaces on smart shoes were a nightmare. One had a friend who broke his collarbone. And it was established that there would usually be cameras but they might not have been installed. There'd been none for months. And it was said that nobody knew the man or had even noticed him before the accident, unless you count noticing that he was tall. And everyone believed it was an accident because his face down there said he never meant it, the poor guy. It was just an awful thing, a surprise to many that it was not a common thing, the way the platforms were so crowded most days. It's bound to happen. And when the police arrived, that's what they got, a room of us, all sad and agreeing, quiet, not crying yet, just wanting to be alone with our loved ones.

ARE YOU DOING ANYTHING LATER? he said eventually, and she said, laughing, *No*. He said, *We could go and get something to eat. Are you hungry?* Uneasy about that, the lights, the menus, she said, *I was going to have something at home*. Then she said, *You can join me if you like*. So now they are in the taxi and her thoughts are of Steph. Two texts she's sent without reply, which could mean anything. Steph could be at Greg's. She could be at home. The taxi could pull in and there could be the blue of television on the curtains, Steph on the sofa, Steph with her sewing stuff out, Steph eating. They'd have to make conversation. Steph would pretend to go to bed.

Patrick's hand is on her knee. He's kissing her again and she responds, the beard startling in the dark. The hand moves along her thigh.

Just a bit further up, she says as the taxi dawdles.

Patrick begins to laugh, and soon she understands. Now she's trying not to laugh as well, or not laugh loudly. They veritably shake, the two of them. She is going to have to tell the driver to stop soon, but doesn't trust herself to speak.

Here, she manages.

Just here?

There's a smile in his voice too.

Yes, she says, relieved.

The house is dark and still.

Patrick passes some notes through the taxi window and says keep the change. She unlocks the front door, and with a finger tells him to wait on the step. A quick search satisfies her that the house is empty. She tidies as she goes.

My housemate, she says when she returns. I wasn't sure if she'd be in.

I live alone, he says.

But it's easier to kiss, and in they stumble. His hands resume before the door is closed. They go underneath her jacket. They cover and contain her. She tries but her arms won't go round him. She's lost in the heat of alcohol and laughter and how long it's been since she had grip on a man.

He lets his jacket fall and she does too. Her shirt she leaves for him. His fingers pick roughly at the buttons until she totters back against a radiator, half undone. He lifts her off the ground with ease. She closes her eyes and feels herself crushed against the wall. Pressing him away with her palms, she forces him to put her down again. She takes his hand and leads him to the stairs, extremely ready.

Are you the same person now that you were a year ago? Or ten years? Just consider it. Consider how you feel. Myself, I find the question peculiarly hard. I can remember things I did, and things I knew, and how I felt, and I suppose I am a changed person, but what does that mean? Can people change and still be themselves? Or does changing change who you are? The question has been asked since Heraclitus at least.

Recklessness is interesting. You'll know the feeling, I expect, when a kind of lust for now swamps all good sense. Who-you-are-now just wants something and that's the end of it, because who-you-are-going-to-be will pay the bill. To me, this suggests that you are different people at those different times, otherwise you would value the feelings of each moment equally. It certainly seems wrong to feel guilty afterwards. You-now can hardly be responsible for the choices you-then made so selfishly. I suppose this may explain guilt's popularity. It holds you together by a thread that you are reluctant to let go.

I have another question. If I had a machine that could instantly and exactly duplicate every particle and energy state in your body, would the copy of you it produced be you as well? It would certainly think it was, since it would have all your memories. Yet I would know which was the original, and it feels to me like that would matter a great deal. You cannot suddenly have two lives, surely? On being told that it had lived only a few seconds, that all its memories were copies, I expect the duplicate of you would be very upset.

Where this leaves us, I think, is having to accept that neither you nor I exist materially. You are neither your mind nor your body. You are your story. Think of yourself as a stack of snapshots taken at every instant of your life, each very like the one above and below it, but no two identical.

That's who you are, not the snapshots themselves but the sequence of them. It's when time drags a finger down the corners that you come to life.

—

One at a time we were taken away to make statements. There was another office across the concourse, which they'd made private by rigging some kind of blanket against the glass. We who were left just watched the escalator running. We saw police and the orange vests of the engineers. A long dark bag was carried up on a stretcher, rather decorously, we knew, for the mess inside. We saw the cleaners going down.

When they finished asking me what I'd seen and making me sign things, the police gave me a leaflet. *Victim Support,* it said, and underneath in cursive script, *We're here to help.* I'm looking at it now. It makes me think. Am I a victim? A subhead answers my question with a question. *Do you need counselling?* Well maybe I did need it, but I didn't feel so then. I felt drugged. I was flying. There was a kind of wildness and escape. I'd taken a not at all calculated risk, but I felt more free than frightened. What I'd done for her, for both of us, it belonged in legend. Like something for the Greeks, or Shakespeare. Besides, I'd lived circumscribed by good sense for many years, and the lack of risk imparts a stealthy kind of drift to life, which is a risk in its own right. Maybe that's why we inoculate ourselves with the synthetic jeopardy of stories. Maybe danger is a food group.

Suffice it to say I've not discussed Will's death with

anyone before now, but I have often contemplated the discussion. I imagine being asked *Why?* and my answer is always that the feeling I found on the station platform doesn't have a name that I know, but it's in the same family as the lure of cliff edges and car accidents. The feeling was strong, and I couldn't help it. I did it for justice, for Frances, for the sake of it, for myself.

I went home. Police said they'd drive me but I said no thanks. I wanted the meander. For several hours I sat on buses thinking about Frances. I wanted to go to her and say what I'd done, but I became tangled by my hesitations. I don't know when I got back. Quite late. I remember putting away the glasses and showering the gel grooves from my hair. I didn't sleep much. I rose early again the next day.

Patrick leans out of bed and fetches cigarettes from among his clothes. He offers them over. He must have been abstaining all this time. The ghost was in his hair. Frances says no thanks. He reaches for his lighter, but the reach becomes a search, conducted in phases marked by thwarted sighs and little groans of effort. She watches the triangle of his hip and shoulder flex in the lamplight, the grid of his ribs.

OK, she says. Give me one, and yelps as the packet flies over.

The lighter at last found, she flicks the lamp off and opens the window, wrapping herself in a counterpane against the cold. He takes her cigarette and lights it in his lips with his. He looks still bigger naked, more serious. They smoke silently for a while, aiming their outbreaths through the curtains.

I know what you should do, he says. You should say you'll tell the client everything, unless you get your job back.

Yes, I've thought about that. It's my nuclear deterrent. But I'd be finished in consulting if I went through with it. I'd probably be finished just by making the threat.

His ember nods and rustles. They fall silent again.

People get sex all wrong, she thinks. It's not an expression of being connected to someone. It's a way for people to connect. Or maybe she's not good at connecting in other ways. Certainly it's rare for her to feel the kind of intimacy, even with good friends, that she feels now in the dark with this naked stranger. Perhaps that's lust's ulterior motive, to lead her here to these calm aftertimes. Perhaps that underlies her liking for haphazard and unsuitable partners. Unsuited to the main part of her life anyway. You don't get this kind of peace with suitable people, people like colleagues or friends, people you have a future with. After sex with them you have silences of other kinds. Of course she can guess what's said about her, and cares not a bit whether the guess is right. All the suitable relationships she sees when she looks around are either patched with compromises or flat. There's romance in the sad brief truth of flings.

I suppose, he begins . . .

Oh forget it. She blows out smoke. Tell me about your business. What do you deliver?

Anything. Anything you can put in a van. A lot of chairs and desks and stuff, for this office supplies company. Books? Architectural models? Design prototypes? That's probably the most interesting. I work with a few architects and designers.

They must really trust you to move stuff like that.

Yeah. I think they do. Obviously you empty the van and strap everything down. I also found this tool that plots a route without speed bumps. Or hardly any.

Clever. How many vans do you operate?

Well, he says, and straight away she knows that it's one. It depends on the job. You don't want lots of vans parked up all the time, costing you tax and interest payments, so I like to keep a small core for regular or short-notice work, with access to more drivers and a bigger fleet when I need it. If I got an order right now that needed fifty vans, I could fill it. No trouble.

Have you looked at the online auctions market?

Not in detail.

It's just that there's still growth in most online sectors. It's demographically driven, so it's pretty secure. Basically old people who don't understand computers are dying all the time and being replaced by people who grew up with them. Most markets are already crowded, but because they are still expanding that creates niches like yours. Fragile goods specialists, I mean.

He is nodding.

If you get on there and position yourself that way, you might find a lot more business, and at a negligible upfront cost. Look at what the competition is charging, if there is a competition, then decide whether you offer a clearly better service, or could do it cheaper. It's probably best to start cheap anyway, while you get the hang of things and people get to know you. Mention the speed bumps. That's great.

Mmm. Thanks.

Back in bed they put their arms around each other. She disengages to find a more comfortable position, then he does, then they go to sleep.

UHF audio and video transmitters are cheap and small but as I may have said they have a limited range. That's why spies and cops in movies have to wait outside in a van. Not being able to wait continuously myself, I had therefore installed some miniature recording devices alongside the transmitters, much as I did with Nina. In order to upload the contents I'd need to visit now and then, like a fisherman checking lobster pots. Thanks to the transmitters however, I could rest against the wheel arch with my headphones on, waiting for someone to wake up. I dozed peacefully.

Shortly before 8.30 a car pulled up beside the van. It paused, then parked behind me. I wound back the video. It was a police car. The doors opened, but instead of knocking on my window or flinging the van open, which I was braced for, the two officers crossed to Frances's doorstep, then pressed the bell.

Thuds. A mechanism. Feet finding rhythm on the stairs.

Frances herself at the door in a dressing gown, sleep's disorder in her hair, its chalk on her skin. Poor thing. Face agape with worry.

They took her to the living room and told her. For a while she said only, *I see.*

More feet on the stairs. Slower ones this time.

Is everything OK?

A man's voice.

No, actually. Someone at work has had an accident. Sorry, can we have a minute?

The police assented. On the kitchen microphone I heard the man say,

Are you OK?

I don't know. It's, um . . . Look, let's talk later. What's your number?

He recited the digits. Patrick from the pub. Then her voice said,

I'll call you so you have mine.

Cool . . . No, hang on, my phone's dead.

OK. Wait a minute. Um. Use that.

Thanks. Sorry but I'm late for a job. I'd better go, OK?

OK. See you.

I hope things work out.

More footsteps.

Sorry about that.

She was back in the front room.

He opened the door in last night's clothes and scanned the street. When you've studied guys like this you learn that furtive and strutting are the two styles. It's either the quick arms and the chin victorious or it's this clownish shrinking out of sight. They always think someone must be watching, they have such admiration for themselves.

The police said that Frances was seen arguing with Will shortly before what they would only call *the incident*.

Out of sight of the house, Patrick's walk got its jostle back.

He'd done her and was thinking, as they do think, young men like him, that sex is theft. It's probably best that we don't have his thoughts in detail, better not to know what Frances was to him. Just remember that one day he'll get his. It's the tragedy of youth, the belief that these are the good times, that they'll soon be over, and the way that the belief itself makes this come true.

That's right. There were some problems at work.

The police said her colleagues mentioned that.

Could you tell us what you remember about his behaviour?

Patrick took a phone out of his pocket and held it to his ear.

Well. We were on the street. We argued actually. As I say, we're going through a bit of a rough patch at the moment. We were. It's complicated. I was angry . . . Sorry, I've literally just got up.

IN THE FRONT ROOM THEY TELL HER what has happened, the fire remnants cold in the grate, a woman and a man. The woman does the talking. She is good at it, quiet and slow, giving each piece its time. To look at, she's all hands in her lap and level eyes and sorrowful resolve like a hangman's. It would be her speciality, the grief knock, a matter of repute down the station and delegated gladly. Frances wonders whether this woman also gave the news to Will's wife Sophie. She thinks of Sophie this morning, gathering the girls.

It appears to have been an accident, the policewoman is saying like it could have been something else. Was Will depressed?

Frances thinks. Was he? She knows they don't always seem it, the depressed, but Will really did seem quite the other way. Maybe he did write the email and knowing he was about to be exposed thought the prospect worse than dying. Had her shouting found its target? It hadn't seemed so. And what would it mean for her? Would she return to work his murderer or his victim? Through the mists of the moment she can't tell. She keeps thinking about his girls.

Is everything OK? Patrick is dressed and leaning in from the hall, leaning not entering.

No, actually. Someone at work has had an accident. Sorry, can we have a minute?

The policewoman agrees and Frances takes Patrick to the kitchen. She has no wish to see him again, but can't summon the bluntness of not swapping numbers. They don't even kiss goodbye. Fifteen hours since they met. Fourteen since Will died. It could be months. Last week was years ago.

When she returns the police ask where she and Will left things. She'd expected some of this. Why else make the trip to tell a colleague? Maybe the man was watching how she took the news. She tells them everything, in a gentle version. Her feelings have softened after all. She asks them to wait while she gets dressed, and brings down the email for them to read.

Where exactly did she go after the dispute with Will?

Back into the pub. To the table with Patrick.

How much longer did she stay there?

An hour or two? A while. I don't know.

Did she leave the pub at all during that time? Maybe get something to eat? Go for a smoke?

I don't smoke. No, I mean. No, I didn't leave.

Is Patrick a friend? A boyfriend? A colleague . . .?

They let the interrogative note hang, to show that of course the endless variability in the types of human relationship cannot possibly be represented by a list of standard terms, and that they're fine with that, because, both as police and despite being police, they celebrate all lifestyles.

It's complicated, she says.

Her feet are cold. Having gone to get dressed, she wonders if it would look evasive to go again for slippers.

They want to know if Patrick spoke to Will or saw him.

No. He stayed inside. I mean he might have seen him through the window . . .

Patrick? they say, and suspend the word again.

You want his surname?

They do, but she knows she doesn't know it. They let her think for a long time, the bastards. She hates them for their tact.

At last they stand, their uniforms rustling. They say they're sorry for bringing such sad news. They thank her for her time. There's no hurry, they say, but if possible they'd like a phone number for Patrick, and maybe his address? She gives them the number she has and they leave theirs in case she thinks of something. The cat suggests breakfast round her shins. She wonders if she should have had a lawyer present.

It's important to keep your distance in these situations, by which I don't mean enough yards of pavement, though it's important to keep those too, but emotions-wise. I learned this the hard way with my seventy-first subject, Evangeline F. She was thirty-four years old, divorced with children, and her boyfriend hit her. You wouldn't know. I didn't know. Whatever his feelings at the time, they never overpowered him to the extent that he hit her in the face. I only discovered what was going on when I overheard one of his apologies on a Sunday morning. We were in a playground, him, Evangeline and me, plus a lot of other people. He went on a great tour of his regrets while the kids took turns on the slide and limping Ange stood silent. You could see that bugged him. With hindsight, he obviously regretted beating her, so now, being sorry, he expected to be forgiven. He thought that's what being sorry got you, and did not at all like being refused. So he kept talking. He kept talking and talking, trying new phrases, new angles, new combinations of old phrases and angles, right through his repertoire of passwords to her anger. He did his best but he was not a patient man. Soon he was on her share of the blame. Ange said nothing. Now and then a child called out to have its exploits witnessed, and she would brighten and congratulate them. Nothing for him. Yet she did not kick him out. That puzzled me until later in the week when, after work, she at last shared her problems with two friends, who had all but guessed already. She said she knew it was what beaten women said, but she did think he was trying to change, and that she owed the kids stability. *They've already lost one dad.* I underlined those words. Her friends did not contradict her. I suspect they were keeping straight faces in order to respond more credibly to any future hints of a changed mind. I watched for hints myself over the weeks that followed, but I didn't see any. I saw more beatings, or their results. It got depressing and I tried a couple of times to move on to other subjects, but I found it hard to concentrate and kept coming back to check on Ange. I'd wait outside her flat, full of hope, then see the way she walked to work, and I'd just know. She looked sadder some times than others. Otherwise nothing changed.

You could only hope that eventually her stoicism would be weaker than her ribs. Then by chance I became aware of a technique the guy was using to inflate his social security payments. For days I agonised over whether to inform the authorities. At last I did, and the guy skipped town. I was delighted, as were the children. They hadn't cared for him at all. But it brought a change in Evangeline. Friends told her she was better off without him, but she didn't see it that way. Pretty soon she was fully depressed, unable to work, neglectful of the children. Worse, when she found out that the guy had a new girl, she became vindictively fixated. She took to making silent phone calls and sending weird things in the post. It was hard to say what she hoped to achieve. By then I don't think her behaviour had reasons you or I would recognise. Now I realise that I'd mistaken her suffering for virtue, which is the kind of moral hallucination that empathy induces if you don't keep properly detached. When you see Patrick leave, and you leave your van to follow him, you must be sturdy. You can't be flotsam on your feelings.

Patrick had mentioned *my company* in the pub the night before. Having boarded a bus, he took a phone call about an appointment later in the day. I got close enough to hear, but the details were elusive. There was talk about types of boxes, and about times, but that could mean anything. I'd not been able to write down the phone number he'd given Frances. At one point in the call he spelled out his email, so I sent him a message.

URGENT request was the subject line. Then, *Hi there. I'm just emailing around for quotes on an urgent job that's coming up in the next few days. Can you tell me what your rates are, and what your capacity is like?*

His phone pinged as the message arrived. I saw him type his answer.

Sure, it said. *Standard is 15 per small item same day within 20 miles. Fragile 30 per item. Longer distances or 50kg+ on request. What's the job? We can handle any size.*

So he was in logistics. This was bad news. Of all the things he could have done, few would be harder to track. Online I found nothing about him. He had a not uncommon surname, which didn't help.

The bus took us through the centre of the city and out into the suburbs. Near the end of the line Patrick got off and led me into a busy road. Large houses with grand porticos and railings topped with paint-plumped spears stood on either side. They would have been fine family homes until the traffic came. Now they were split into flats, and the once-white stucco was looking powdery. You could tell the road was known to Patrick from the direct way he walked, without regard for pedestrian crossings. This being a weekday morning, you'd expect him to be busy, and when suddenly he hoisted himself into a van I was ready to watch him drive away. Instead he climbed back out with a plastic bag he'd found and headed down the steps of a basement flat. As I walked past I heard him whistling while he hunted for his keys.

Frances roams the house for hours, her mind churning, her hands hungry for work. She checks her emails, checks the news, changes her sheets. Her mother rings but she doesn't answer. She sends Patrick a text to say sorry for the morning, and mentions that the police may call. At eleven she is hungry and eats a bowl of cereal and a box of pasta salad out of sequence. Afterwards she showers. Dressing, she sees that Patrick has replied. *who is this?* the message says. *Frances,* she writes back, perplexed. *sorry wrong number don't no a frances :-)* Yet it is the number Patrick gave.

Others will have seen her in the pub, of course. That's not in question, given the spectacle she made. She remembers a tall barman with dark hair, and a yellow T-shirt deliberately small for him. He was about to serve her when she ran out to confront Will. He is sure to remember.

Rattling in on the train she gets a text from Tim. He is telling her the news, in case she hadn't heard. By text. That's Tim. He reckons Will's death supersedes the ban on them talking, and suggests they meet for lunch. She agrees.

The Rising Sun is open when she gets there. Young staff slap mops around the floor and fill the fridges from the back. Windows are open and a breeze tries to drag away the beery air. It also drags in dabs of rain. There's music on. Nobody is talking. They do not look up when Frances enters. A girl with many piercings and a streak of blue in her hair comes over when it is clear that no one else will.

Can I help?

Hi. I don't know if you remember me? I was here last night.

Sorry, I wasn't working last night.

No. Fine. It's actually one of your colleagues I'm looking for. A tall thin guy with black hair. Do you know who I mean?

Carsten?

Possibly. I don't know.

It sounds like Carsten. He's the deputy manager. Can I ask what this is about?

Of course, yes. It's a bit unusual, really. Nothing important. I just want to find someone I met here. Or I might want to, anyway. Can I talk to Carsten? Is he around?

He might be in the office.

She goes to check. Her incuriosity about the details is almost hurtful. Is it their different ages? Does Frances look too old to be imagined in an intrigue? Too old to be imagined altogether? She doesn't think she's aged much, but that's probably how it starts, with younger people growing blind to your affairs.

At length Carsten appears, and he is indeed the thin man that she remembers. She smiles.

How can I help you?

He could be anything from Swiss to Norwegian. Last night he'd been inaudible.

Hi. I was in here yesterday with a friend. You served me, do you remember? You were going to serve me anyway.

Carsten studies her.

I was next in the queue but ran out before my turn. You saw me, then I came back and the man I was with got drinks.

He takes a step back and inclines his head.

We were sitting at that table right there. We were there all evening. I'd been here since before six, in office clothes. A dark suit with a white shirt. The guy, his name's Patrick. Maybe you've seen him before? He's quite big, tall, with a beard. Like a short beard, you know. Trimmed short.

Glenn?

Patrick. He has a leather jacket. He was wearing a leather jacket. Big guy. Young. Well, you know, probably in his mid-twenties.

Slow at first, then resolutely, Carsten shakes his head.

But we were here all night! Right in front of you. You must remember.

I believe you. But it was busy, you know. We serve a lot of people. Things get kind of blurry.

Try to remember. I ran off when you were about to get my drinks. I pushed people out of my way. I shouted at someone outside, then came back. I'd bought another drink earlier on, another gin and tonic.

Yes, I remember someone running out. Maybe it was you, but I did not see you come back again. From me you bought your drink?

No, I don't think that was you. That was someone else, earlier. I don't know who.

It is easy to forget these things, you see.

Yes, but the point is I was here afterwards, for most of the evening.

Well, I was not. I came in only for the early shift.

That doesn't matter. You were about to serve me. It was definitely you. You caught my eye. It was only a minute later when I came back in.

She wonders why she is not more memorable.

Can I ask what this is about?

Do you have CCTV here, anything like that?

No. I don't think so. Is it important?

Can you really not remember me? Imagine I'm wearing a dark suit.

She stands back from the bar so he can see her fully. She sits where she sat.

This is the table. I was here all night until about eleven. Are you sure you don't have CCTV? Go and check.

Some of the others are becoming interested.

I believe you, sure. I just can't say I remember.

She is waiting in the nasty place Tim named. She's shaken the water off her coat, although it's only going to be rained on again afterwards, she knows, the way it's looking, there's that evenness about the sky and in the distribution of drops, settled rain you'd call it, the work of methodical clouds. She searches for *Patrick delivery* on her phone. Then *Patrick logistics*. Then *Patrick fragile*. Then *Patrick van*. Then other things, because losing hope is the next job on her list. In the end, of course, she believes, in this day and age, with social media and everything, and cameras everywhere, in the end, that he'll be found. If she needs him. Because that's the point here. Yes. That's what she must not forget. This is only insurance. She's not in actual trouble. It's just alarming contemplating trouble on this scale. Obviously that'll make you worry, and of course when you worry you're full of anxious energy, so you want to do useful things, which makes what you do feel worth worrying about, whereas the big picture is you're fine. She's fine.

Well it's certainly pulling in business in the bad weather, this restaurant is, if it deserves the dignity of the name. One by one people are coming in and standing wiping their lenses, the people wearing glasses. Often they block the doorway and have to be muttered aside, but still they stand and stare at the illustrated and illuminated menu boards, taking their time. It must be a tough choice. The place serves more or less all food. There are aromas of: scampi, chicken madras, prawn laksa, steak pie, pork generally. The closest she can get to a vegetable is cheese. She has water. She isn't hungry. How funny to come in and buy a bottle of what she's sheltering from. That is ironic. She takes her phone out of her bag and puts it back again. When she's done here she should just go home and have a run, despite the rain. You sweat anyway. Then watch a movie or read her book.

Hey!

Tim sits next to her with an illicit grin, not even a gesture of the proper solemnness.

Hi Tim.

We've just had this long meeting with the top brass, everyone in the company. It took forever.

It's not Tim to say he's sorry.

Have you eaten? he says.

I had something before I left.

I'll just be a minute.

He makes his own inspection of the menus while he stands in line. Frances watches a little heatedly. She didn't mind the first wait, but feels slighted by this encore. At last he comes back with a box of rice and a ladleful of something glistening.

So how about all this? he says, eating. Poor old Will.

It's just awful.

It is.

How is everybody taking it?

A mixture. I haven't seen anyone really upset, but the whole atmosphere is weird. Kind of like the last day of term? No one's getting any work done. They're just wandering around and talking to each other about it. Then when someone arrives who hasn't heard yet, there's this rush to tell them and it all starts up again. How did you find out?

Oh, I got a message this morning. Sounds like a good time for me to be at home, then?

I suppose. It is terrible what happened, obviously, but it's quite interesting to see the office like this.

His poor children, and Sophie. I can't decide if I should write to them. I'm trying not to think about what they're going through, to be honest.

At least Will won't have suffered. I mean a train finishes you off like that. That's why people do it.

You think he chose this?

Maybe. No one is quite saying it, but they want to hear what we think, you and me and Monica. You know, about how he was. A lot of people are asking where you are. I've just said you're working at home since ComPex. That might have upset him, I suppose, losing that. You actually saw him last night, didn't you? There was a bit of a scene? Some of the others said they heard shouting.

Yes. There was a bit of a scene. I feel terrible about it now. I wasn't happy about how he's handling this email business. How he was handling it. God, that seems so trivial now.

I couldn't sit still in the taxi back from Patrick's. I'd shift my ankle to my knee, drop it down, jiggle, scratch, lean forwards. My thoughts did laps. There was ringing in my ears. I wanted the darkness and confinement of the van.

Climbing in at last and putting the headphones on, I heard her soft sounds and felt better. Soon afterwards the front door opened. Frances was dressed casually today, in tight grey jeans and a blue coat. She looked wonderful, but her walk was tense. She vanished in the direction of the station. Hearing no further sounds I crossed the road and rang the bell as before, scanning the glass for any fleck of movement. Seeing none, I entered.

The first recording device was stuck underneath the kitchen table, hidden by a drawer whose obduracy had a day earlier been comforting, but was now a headache. As I lay on my back trying to reach it with the data cable I realised I'd left the replacement batteries in the van. I swore. Without new batteries, some of the devices might not see out the afternoon, but I could not keep going back and forth across the road to fetch them. They would have to wait for next time.

The second device was taped to the back of a high bookshelf in the sitting room, which meant removing the books in front of it, and doing this with the curtains open, because I did not dare get close to the windows. Again the data uploaded smoothly, I was glad to see.

The third device I'd wedged into the space between smoke alarm and baseplate on the ceiling of the landing. I brought up a kitchen chair, but removing the alarm was a stretch, and afterwards I struggled to put it back. Something about the twisting action meant that I couldn't apply enough upward pressure to get the threads to latch. Time and again I'd pull away thinking I'd done it, and the alarm would stay in my hand. A couple of times I nearly dropped it. Perhaps the day before I'd had a slightly higher chair. At last I went foraging. There had to be a ladder somewhere to reach the loft hatch, but I couldn't find it. Instead I came back with a cushion of Stephanie's, which I hoped would raise me just enough. I did not think to take account of its slipperiness on the wooden seat, however, and as a result when I stood on it and reached upwards the cushion shot back towards the room I'd fetched it from, sending me the other way. Exactly what happened then I don't know. I imagine I clawed the air a bit, one foot still touching the chair and causing it to pitch sideways, landing my weight full on one corner along the angle of the leg. There was that wrench that wood makes, then it gave way. The bathroom door-jamb clipped me on the cheek as I tried to shield the smoke alarm on the way down.

At this point I had two problems, besides pain. First, the alarm still had to be attached, for which I'd need another chair and the cushion again. I felt I would have the required height if I was careful, and indeed this time the alarm went in. The second problem was more difficult. As things stood, Stephanie and Frances would discover on their return that a chair of theirs had broken inexplicably. My first thought was to smuggle away the evidence, an absent chair seeming somehow less mysterious than a smashed one. Briefly I even believed that the housemates might forget how many chairs they had. They were ordinary chairs. Keeping two in the front room and three in the kitchen suggested a set of six already down by one, as well as some haziness over their distribution. Once the cushion and the new chair were put away, however, I decided I could neither take the chance of the chair being missed, nor of being seen carrying it. I therefore had two options: to mend it discreetly or to arrange it broken. Instinctively I preferred the second, which would be faster, though it had drawbacks. Did apparently sound wooden chairs, on rare occasions, spontaneously reject their own legs? Could I give it the appearance of having suffered from some stealthy but calamitous dry rot? The damage did not look like rot. Two support struts were out of their sockets and each stump where the leg had broken was a brush of splinters. I tried to artfully disarray the pieces on the kitchen floor in the manner of an accident. A bread machine sat on a high shelf above the table, evidently not much used, which might, when placed at the centre of the mess, be made to seem the author of it. But was the machine heavy enough? When I picked it up I didn't think so. Plus there were worries about the angle of attack. To seem authentic, the machine would also need some damage. I momentarily considered pulling the whole shelf down, then chose mending. Clearly, even with time and the correct tools, I could not return the chair to its original condition, probably not even to robustness. Instead my idea was to attempt a repair solid enough to hold, but at the same time ready to collapse beneath whoever sat on it, thereby causing them an accident to mask my own. In fact, by reinserting the supports into their holes and enmeshing the pieces' ends, this could be rigged up almost naturally. After some gentle malleting with a saucepan, the chair was even strong enough for me to sit on, gingerly. The break was high on the leg, so you had to lift the chair or crouch in order to see it. I myself was in this pose when a cat approached, purring, not a bit alarmed. I gave it a few strokes then hurried to my final device, a tiny video camera fixed behind a plastic grille that ventilated the chimney breast in Frances's bedroom. At last with some relief I crossed the road, the sky low, dark spots appearing on the asphalt, and drove home with the wipers on.

I think I planned to review my recordings later, after a nap. I knew that I was tired. These were early mornings and full days that I was living through and I'm telling you I was pretty much down to my body's vapours. I was in that trembly hyperactive stage when you can't pause or you'll collapse. Whatever I planned, I know what I did. I watched the video immediately.

A quiet beginning, Frances getting changed, her body slightly fisheyed by the camera, its decisions over these shoes, that blouse, round but plain. After she leaves the room there are three minutes, three programmed empty minutes while the camera waits for movement, and I waited too. You watch the clothes through the slightly open door of her wardrobe. You watch the clothes cooling on the floor. It's yours, this time. Yours, not even borrowed or stolen. Then it's what you knew was coming. Knew but had to check. A flick to darkness and a slot of light, then through it stagger the lovers. There'd been a hope, though not one you put weight on, of spying some resistance or reluctance in her, maybe a detectably grim resolve to get this done. Well that is dead now. This is more than willing, how she grasps at his clothes, and into them, and how she gives herself to be stripped. She must have been eager, given how fast they find their stride under the sheets. It's been vilely clear for a while how eager he is. Now you can hear them. The camera has a microphone, though weak. You hear that she is the more vocally exuberant, as is customary. She counts out her satisfaction with his work, which by degrees removes the covers. Her face you can't see. It will be somewhere underneath his shoulder cords. There are some licks of hair. His face, eyes closed, you have only a thin crescent of. Where he's stuck her it's just a great black mass. Mainly the rest is pulling hands and leg spasms and the bulbing of his buttocks in your lens.

She's walking through the rain, collar up, hair soaked to a glaze. Most people have umbrellas. That's how wise most people are. And most who don't are in taxis, or crowded under bus shelters, or greying windows with their breath. Her bag buzzes.

Hi Steph. Hang on a second.

She presses herself into the porch of a bankrupt shop.

Sorry Steph. It's pissing down. I meant to get back to you last night, and I got your texts, thanks so much. I don't know where to start. It's been such a horrible day.

Let me start then.

OK.

Guess what?

What?

Me and Greg are getting married!

How arduous she finds it, how heavy, to say in the right tone,

That's wonderful! Congratulations!

Yay! Thank you! His case finished yesterday, so we went for dinner last night and he just came out and asked me!

Wow. That's fantastic, Steph! I'm so pleased for you!

She says this because it is true. It is nice to have some happiness around.

I sort of knew it was coming, because he'd booked this place we really like. Passeggiata. You know it? We usually discuss where we're going, but he just suddenly announced we had a table there, so I was quite keyed up. I was like, haha, I was watching all the waiters like a total hawk, convinced he'd prepared something, you know, like when they put the ring in the blancmange, even though I know that isn't really Greg's style.

No. Definitely.

But in the end he just pulled out a box during the pudding. It was a while before I noticed, actually, I'm such a space cadet. I was busy eating, and rabbiting on about these costumes. I think I'd stopped expecting it by then. So it was only when I realised that he wasn't talking that I looked down and saw the box. Then he asked me! He didn't go down on one knee or anything, but actually I'm glad. The place was really full. It would have been so embarrassing!

What's the ring like?

Oh it's *gorgeous*. A really simple platinum band, with a half-carat lemon diamond. You know how I've always loved lemon diamonds?

Beautiful. So have you made any plans?

Well, we're thinking Ireland. Greg has family there, and it's got some beautiful places that are quite cheap right now. Next summer on the west coast is probably what we'll aim for. Maybe the year after.

Oh well, it's really great news. I'm so happy for you, Steph. Will you be home later? We must celebrate!

We must! And you must tell me your news. How did it go yesterday? What's been horrible?

Frances explains. She tries to sound calm.

Oh my God, that's awful, Steph says at last.

A large crowd is sheltering in a sandwich shop across the road.

Frances?

She is thinking of that other man. The nice man from the Rose Cafe. He was in the pub. She'd clean forgotten. He'd seen her after she came back in, then spoken to Patrick on his way out about some client. A publisher, that's right. The man has her number. He would definitely remember.

Frances?

She is walking. The publisher would have a number for Patrick. She needs to remember their name.

Sorry, Steph. It's pouring here. Look, I'm so happy about your news. It's really wonderful. I'll see you at home soon, OK? You must have loads more people to tell.

She skips across the road and takes a long route to avoid the office. What was the client's name? She lands a step on a loose stone and takes a splash on the ankle. These lesser streets don't get the love of the thoroughfares. She finds the Rose Cafe, but he isn't there. She collects herself. She knows that he's a regular. He told her so. She buys tea again and sits at the same table. She mops her hair with a handful of napkins, and hangs up her coat to dry. She gets out her book. Her breaths lengthen and her shoulders wilt. Rain chatters against the glass, but she doesn't hear. She is lost, her legs are crossed. The tea goes cold. The words draw her in, as fire draws air.

SATURDAY MORNING AND THE SOUND of keys. *Hello!* Steph sings. Frances wades down to her in slippers. They embrace. Steph shows the ring.

I'm sorry, she says. I know it's been a hideous week for you, but I'm still dizzy at the moment. I can't believe it. I've hardly even slept.

No, it's wonderful. Honestly, it's just the news I need. Have you had breakfast?

Steph hasn't, so feeling festive they begin a hunt for the teapot, but instead come across the stovetop coffee maker and half a bag of beans long since folded and forgotten. They feed the lot through the grinder. And there's bread and eggs. They decide to have homemade lattes with buttered toast and the eggs scrambled. As they cook they remember the chats they've had about marriage over the years, and the chats generally, even the times they joked about the chat they're having now. The young sun patterns them with next door's leaves. They stir the eggs and assemble the machine and laugh, and now and then lean on the counter. The food is ready first, so they eat it beside the coffeepot. Their thoughts touch upon the strangeness of eating cooked food standing, a hand for a table, a fork pressed and waggled as a knife. It's only a touch because they don't want the nonchalance of the moment spoiled. It implies that they are independent young women who so often spend mornings eating homemade food with friends that it's done casually. Being intent on their nonchalance, however, they forget the coffee, which is billowing wildly when they lift the lid. To cool it they add too much milk, which at least mitigates the tastes of staleness and scalding. They say how good it is, and hide from the lie in a discussion of where Stephanie will live.

He's planning to sell when the market's better.

To go where?

Just anywhere we can get more space. Probably a bit further out. You don't want to jinx it, but I suppose we'll be looking for a family home.

Stephanie puts her mug on the table.

When do you expect to move out?

Probably next month. Maybe before. Like you said I'm almost living with him already. There's more of my stuff in his flat than his! I'll just take the rest in batches.

Is there a date we could pencil in? It's just that if I'm going to find a new housemate, they'll want to know when they can have the room.

Oh. Well it can be quite soon, if you like. Shall we say two weeks from now?

Sooner than Frances had expected. Sooner than any tenancy agreement would allow.

Whoever moves in, you know they'll never replace you, she says.

Ah thanks. I was thinking that if . . .

Stephanie sits and the chair twists sharply, holds long enough for her to look up, confused, then collapses, tipping her forwards on to the floor. She sits resplendent in the pieces. Laughter takes Frances over. She can't speak. All her strength goes into safely putting down the cup that she can no longer hold. A hand supports her on the table while fresh hilarities come to her in spasms. There's the counter-majesty of Stephanie's neat placement in the mess. There's the apt timing of the accident, as though fate had heard their conversation about klutzy Stephanie being irreplaceable and given prompt supporting evidence. There's the exact irony that Stephanie was sitting down to get all serious, trying to physically reflect the businesslike direction of their talk, and that this put her on the floor. There's also the desire to laugh for any reason. Life lacks laughs just now. Plus this pratfall takes Steph's cultivated girlishness and snaps its stems. She wants this emphasised without being seen to emphasise it herself, and does this with laughter, helpless laughter. There's been a lot of Frances being right about Steph in the past year and not much of anybody noticing. A crumb of justice is worth all her chairs. When the laughs wane she stokes them further until she sees that Steph has had enough.

It just went, Steph says, standing. I barely touched it.

Through the last chuckles,

I'll take it out of your deposit.

Don't you dare. Honestly, I am sorry but it just went.

Oh don't worry. It doesn't matter. Those chairs are pretty old.

They address the mess. One takes the swinging skeleton, the other the detached leg and crosspiece. With nowhere else to leave them, they leave them in the back corner of the front room. When they return their coffees are too cold to enjoy.

So do you think you'll see this guy again? The guy you brought home?

Patrick.

Yes. Is he good news? If you find him, I mean?

Steph is an inveterate matchmaker and basically deaf about it, deaf or wilful. Years back she had a passion for arranging double dates, which Frances wanly outlasted. Accepting now that she is unable to help in this regard Steph keeps help in readiness. Instead of loud zeal there is now loud forbearance, which breaks at any mention of new lovers, any hint of an escape for Frances from the spinsterhood that her warmer-blooded housemate has been spared.

Anyway, Frances says.

She is sorting through books in her room cross-legged when the police call. It is a gentle-voiced DI Someone, whatever a DI is. He says there is no news. He says,

I'm trying to get hold of Patrick. It is Patrick, isn't it? The man you spent Thursday evening with?

Yes.

Do you have his correct phone number?

No, I don't. Actually I meant to say I think the number he gave me isn't right. I texted yesterday and it's not him.

I've had the same trouble. Do you have an email address instead? Or just a surname?

No. I'm sorry. I know he has a small delivery business, but I don't know what it's called. He might just be a sole trader. He often works for architects, he said. And publishers and designers.

Thank you. I'm sure we'll find him if we need to.

Do you know yet what happened to Will?

I can't discuss specific details of the investigation.

No of course.

But I want to assure you that we have a team working on it, that's partly why I rang. At the moment we're approaching the incident with an open mind. This is important so we can collect good evidence for the coroner or any courts. It's vital for the family to have confidence in the courts' conclusions.

The words sound read out. She imagines them being typed somewhere.

Of course. It's such an awful thing. I wish I could do more to help.

My colleagues said you were very helpful yesterday. In fact, that's something else I want to ask about. I believe you visited the Rising Sun pub late yesterday morning? Or perhaps early afternoon?

I did, yes. I was trying to find Patrick actually.

Yes. I was there later myself and some of the staff mentioned it. You were agitated, is that right?

Well, no. Not agitated. No, that isn't right. I was frustrated. I was trying to find Patrick. I'd just realised that the number was wrong and I was trying to help, because I knew you wanted to talk to him.

It's OK. I understand. Several of the bar staff said you

were eager to find him, and that you wanted them to remember seeing you together.

I didn't *want* them to. I mean, of course I did want that, but I wasn't trying to *make* them remember. I wasn't trying to *force* anybody.

I'm sorry. I phrased that badly. You were trying to jog their memories, let's say.

Yes. I was. I found it hard to believe they had all forgotten. I still find it hard to believe, to be honest. We were there all evening.

That must have been frustrating. And of course people's memories are unreliable. We see that a lot in my work, especially when a case comes to court. The things that people remember change from day to day. That's why I wanted to reassure you that my team can handle it. I appreciate that you want to help, but we are talking to all the relevant people, and it's better for the investigation if you let us interview them first.

Of course. But I mean I wasn't . . .

I understand. It's just important not to do anything that might look like interfering. In some people's eyes.

Listen, I promise you. It was never my intention to interfere in any way.

I know. I thought it best to be sure. Things can easily get misunderstood. I've seen it a few times. Anyway, you have my number I believe? Just get in touch if you remember anything else.

She sits silently on the bed for a long time, then checks a few things on her phone.

Stephanie is in her own room, dividing costumes and

equipment into piles and listening to music.

I'm off out for a bit, Frances says.

OK. I'm about to go out myself.

The cafe is open when Frances arrives. The scowling woman still mans the buns, not so many buns today. Perhaps she depends on even the thin Saturday trade. Perhaps she has nowhere else to go.

In the corner sits a man so round that he could be thirty or fifty. The same man who was here the first time? Frances isn't sure of that either. He is hiding from the aftermath of his breakfast behind a newspaper, his coat still on. Would that be laziness? The coat? It would not be cold. Maybe being so large and alone and thinking little of oneself dulls the feeling of deserving comfort. Self-loathing makes a virtue of self-neglect. Maybe taking off your coat in a small space becomes conspicuous and embarrassing when you go above a certain size. Whatever the truth is, he looks settled in it, with his paper. He sits stone-still but for his brows, which scurry over the letters' rooftops, shuddering across w's and m's, vaulting every chimneyed t. He'll be a regular for sure.

And time does seep by. She's never bored, not with her book and the passing trade and the internet on her phone. She quite forgets her mission until lunchtime, which was when the writer came before, though only for a coffee and a doughnut, which he hardly ate. People who aren't the writer arrive, quite a few people but never in more than twos. They are not manual labourers today, but office workers, office overworkers, sent here on Saturdays by the upscale chains being closed. Some you can see like bad food when no one's looking. Frances plays a game while they queue, trying to predict their orders, and loses nearly always. When she becomes hungry herself she has a jacket potato with strands of cheese and an etiolated side salad. Her orange juice is glugged dispassionately from a box. Only when most people have left does she use the toilet. The door directly adjoins the room and is almost cardboard. The lock is just a slender hook-and-eye.

Are you all right? the owner asks as they near closing. She has a look that says she has her theories.

Yes thanks. I'm waiting for somebody. I'm just not sure when he'll arrive.

THE BACK OF THE VAN WILL BE packed with yesterday's shopping and you'll be in the front. You'll have brought one large tarpaulin, six rolls of heavy-duty duct tape, ten metres of ten-millimetre climber's rope, a pack of ten large plastic cable ties, a hollow plastic garden parasol stand, a box of surgical gloves, a box of surgical shoe covers, a box of surgical masks, a box of surgical caps, a box of large disposable overalls, two small vials of GHB (gamma hydroxybutyrate), a roll of twenty-five clinical waste bags, fifty heavy-duty refuse sacks, a large sports holdall, a packet of assorted bandages, a large tool box containing a hammer, a mallet, small and large chisels, small and large saws, a carving knife, a boning knife, a cleaver, kitchen scissors, a blowtorch, spare gas and a cigarette lighter, three large sponges, one ten-pack of kitchen sponge-scourers, a fifteen-litre plastic bucket, a four-pack of kitchen towel, six large bathroom towels, two packets of baby wipes, unscented, one ruled notebook and a packet of four ballpoint pens. You'll have decided to wear the glasses again, this time with a beanie hat, hoping it makes you look incurious and low-skilled. You'll be parked quite close to the front door today. You'll listen to her sheets until the streetlights give way to the sun. When she's quiet you'll play some of your best recordings of her, which you keep on your phone.

You'll know that you will audit these hours later in order to explain them to yourself. You'll go over your plan thoroughly, change none of it, but give yourself at least the thoroughness to recall. In any case you'll know that if you do regret what you are about to do, regret can be a phase. You used to regret making Frances suffer with your impetuous email until you realised that her suffering had helped you understand and made you care. Plus you'll have started to believe that thanks to your accusations she is on the road to something better. Being hurt is good for people sometimes. So is hurting others. Plan a painless life and you only season life's pain with disappointment. Better to let yourself flow. Be spontaneous. Make pain count.

Stephanie will pull up in a minicab. She'll pay the driver and open the front door and call *Hello!* into the hall. Presently she'll be met by Frances and they'll start talking about Stephanie's engagement, which naturally excites them. They'll begin work on breakfast.

The next thing on your list will be to email Patrick, cancelling the job you booked him for this morning. Then you'll drive over and ring his doorbell. He'll come to the door and look at you and say,

Can I help you?

Like young men do, all tough.

Hi, you'll say. Listen, I'm sorry to bother you. I'm sure you're busy.

I am, yes.

I want to talk to you about Frances.

Who?

Frances. I'm, well, I'm a close friend of hers. We met briefly in the pub the other day, you and me. She introduced us.

Oh yes.

You're Patrick, aren't you? You run a delivery company? She spoke to you about trying to develop it online?

That's right.

Sorry. This is delicate, but it's important. Do you have a minute?

Now?

If possible.

You'll get a waft of smoker's air.

OK. Come in.

And you'll see why they went to hers. There'll be a sparse bright kitchen at the rear of the flat, and what must be a bathroom and a bedroom, but the rest will be dismal. Packing boxes everywhere and milky little windows gathering what light they can from above ground. It'll be like some lower mammal's burrow, an ashtray and a laptop on the rug showing where he nests. Perhaps ashamed, perhaps seeing you looking, he will take the centre of the leather sofa and hang his arms off his knees to display how big and relaxed he is. The armchair will be yours.

OK, you'll say, like you're nervous. I'm not sure how well you and Frances know each other?

Not at all, really.

OK. Well, basically, she's quite a complicated person. She's been hurt a lot.

Uh-huh.

He knows how that goes.

The truth is I'm not just a close friend of hers, I'm also kind of her boyfriend. We don't live together, but we've been seeing each other for nearly a year.

Right.

He'll look tense.

So before I go any further, I need to say that I know you two spent the night together on Thursday, and that it's OK with me. I expect you didn't know about the situation between us. And she's not exactly . . . Well, that's what I want to talk to you about.

He won't move or speak.

I'm not here to make trouble. I'm here because I'm worried about her, and because there's something that you need to know. Do you and Frances plan to see each other again?

We didn't make any plans.

He'll light a cigarette.

Sure, you'll say. And actually, it's none of my business really. The thing is that over the past year, well, over the past two really, anyway for a long time, she has been getting kind of obsessed with having a baby. She really wants to have a baby. We have talked about it a lot. I'm not totally against the idea, but I am definitely against doing it now. There are various reasons for that. Our relationship needs to be more stable, mainly. She doesn't agree, but I don't think she's really listening. She came off the pill a few months ago, which I said was a bad idea. So that was a worry. I don't know if you discussed it? She won't talk to me about it at all. She's acting like everything is fine, but I can see that things aren't right. She'll say she's going somewhere in the evening, but when I call she'll be somewhere else. Or like, I might suggest coming round to hers, just in a casual way, and she'll be violently against it, saying she is having a *girls' night in* or something, which isn't like her. Obviously I started to wonder if she was seeing someone else, or other people, and of course I had an idea why she might do that. Can I ask? You don't have to tell me if you don't want to, but can I ask, did you and she use any contraception?

He'll stare, smoking and thinking, then say he doesn't know.

I'm afraid that doesn't surprise me. Look, I'm sorry. This must be a shock, but I thought you had a right to know, especially if this was going to continue.

OK, well, you've done it now. You've told me.

He'll stare at your cheek.

What happened to your face?

Oh, I fell off a chair. Look, you probably want to get rid of me, and I don't enjoy coming here, but we need to talk about this.

She's not going to be pregnant, mate.

Probably not. I agree with you. But I don't think it's a long shot. From what I can tell she may have chosen Thursday quite carefully.

I don't think so. She was in the pub because she'd just finished some big meeting at her office. She went and yelled at her boss when he went past.

That meeting was a month ago.

What?

That big meeting. It happened a month ago. The one

about the email and the investigation and all that? Is that what she was talking about? Well it's true, but it wasn't on Thursday. That was five weeks ago or something. She's been off work for ages, and really not been herself. I thought she might be hanging around the office again, maybe keeping tabs on Will, which is why I followed her to the pub.

But I spoke to her. She didn't approach me.

You think she doesn't know how to get approached? You think you're the first man who tried?

He'll say nothing.

If things, you know, I mean if Thursday was a deliberate day for her, and if it has gone how she hoped, then we have a problem. I see her a lot so I might be able to find out. And I might be able to convince her to reverse it, if I agree to have a child with her myself, or maybe just move in. That might be her plan. But we'll need to work together. Can I make tea or something? This is a lot to take in.

I'll make tea, he'll say.

You'll join him in the kitchen.

I mean it's definitely possible I'm being paranoid about all this. Actually, you'll laugh, I hope I am! My own friends say I'm crazy to stay with her, but I think this has been building for a long time, since long before we met. I'm trying to get her to start counselling. Once she has a new career I think that will help. Then maybe we can settle down. She often says that's what she wants, for us to get married, but when we talk we end up back on babies again. Did she seem strange to you?

Not really. I mean she shouted at that guy, but who can blame her?

No, sure. He's been exploiting her for a while, and losing her job was a big shock. Although I do wonder what really went on. I only have her word for most of it, and as you've seen she's a good liar.

How many sugars?

None.

He'll drop two in his.

GHB is famous among pharmacologists for the steepness of its dose-response curve, meaning there's only a narrow ledge between not noticing and hospital. Obviously you'll have tried a small amount on yourself. You'll have found it salty, fast-acting then fast-fading, a fun variation on alcohol's vague glide. You'll also have spent a long time studying dosages and decided that the important thing in this instance, more important than the risk of overdose, is the rapidity and strength of the effect, so you'll have prepared two triple helpings. That should do it, even with a body mass like Patrick's. You'll have one vial in your right pocket with the cap unscrewed.

What's your name again?

You'll lie and he'll spoon out the bags, fetch milk from the fridge and fold his cigarette into a foil tray, splitting the stuffing. You'll take your mug back into the lounge. His has some cartoon on it you can't read. Yours is paisley-patterned.

So you want me to back off, he'll say. Is that what this is?

You'll have to be careful sitting now that the vial's open, or it will spill down your leg.

Sorry?

You've come to tell me that Frances is your girlfriend and

you want me to fuck off. That's basically what you're saying.

No. No. That isn't it. I just want to look after her, and I kind of assume you don't want to have a baby with someone you just met?

But you and her, you are together? Seriously?

Yes. This is not an easy time for us, but yes, just about.

I mean, this is none of my business or anything, but if I were you I'd be angrier right now. I'd want to fucking hurt me.

This'll feel threatening even in the hypothetical. His capacity and his willingness to hurt, that will be clear. You'll be meek.

Well, you'll say. I feel differently. Sorry, but it's true.

Don't apologise, mate. It's me who should be sorry.

You didn't know. I can't blame you. And Frances is having a hard time.

Hard time or not, don't you think there might be other reasons why she's putting herself about?

Such as?

He'll sip his tea, and you'll regret your words. A timid *Like what?* would have been better. Or a plain *What do you mean?* By comparison *Such as?* sounds arch, sceptical, a blood-heater, tactical goading, a proffered chin.

I mean maybe if you stood up for yourself a bit more? Could you do that? Maybe she wants to see you be a man? Maybe that's why she's got a bit vivacious?

He'll give you an implying stare.

Maybe, he'll say. That's all I'm saying.

You might be right. Is that how she was with you?

Mate, it was how it always is.

He gulps more tea. From the inclination of the cup you guess he's about half done.

May I ask, you said you were in logistics?

That's right.

Do you have a card?

What?

A business card.

Er . . . yeah. But what's that got to do with this?

Sorry, it's stupid, but there's this guy I know. He's a fruit wholesaler and he's always looking for drivers at short notice. Do you deliver fruit?

Fruit? Fuck, I deliver anything.

Good, it's just a thought. Would you mind me giving him your card, if you've got one?

Seriously?

He'll laugh, stand up, and go to the bedroom. You'll take the vial out of your pocket and tip it into his drink. Some of it will stream down the cup wall, so you'll swill the whole thing round, trying to get it all into that last inch where you hope his sugar will disguise the saltiness. He'll return to find you staring at a movie poster on the wall, a little stack in his hands, still laughing.

Give these to whoever you like.

Thanks, you'll say. So listen, I need to know everything you remember about your time with Frances.

Why?

I don't know. I mean I don't know what I'm looking for, but I need to hear everything you remember, in case some of it is helpful when I talk to her.

Listen, mate. He'll drain his tea. You'll blink. Listen, I don't know what's going on with you and her, and I don't want to know. Me and her, it was just one of those things. I wasn't planning on seeing her again. I don't think I've got her number. So for now, let's leave it at that, eh? I'm not going to go into it all. If she gets pregnant, and you can prove it's mine, well, then we'll talk.

But that's what I mean. If she gets pregnant, no one will be able to prove anything without her agreeing to it, and even then we might have to wait for the baby to be born. I could maybe talk her into a termination if I knew a bit more about Thursday.

Why? What difference will that make?

I don't know. Maybe none. But we need all the help we can get.

This isn't *we*, OK? You don't want Frances to have another guy's kid. That's fine. But seriously, I'm not getting involved.

And it'll be true. He won't talk, about this or anything. You'll appraise the cards he's given you, their lettering, their print quality, and he'll just laugh. When you start on about the difficulty of running a small business, he'll become solemn and stand. You'll tell him how much you love the movie on his poster, but he'll make it clear he only likes it passingly and start giving you looks. You'll become angry. You'll want to start early, but instead you'll put your head in your hands and pretend you're hiding sadness.

Sorry. It's just. This whole thing . . .

His answer will be to touch the door handle.

She's not going to be pregnant, mate. Chances must be

one in a thousand. It took some courage coming round, but please, I've got stuff to do.

At this point you'll almost feel as though you could start crying.

Of course, you'll say. Sorry. Just give me a moment.

You'll get a tissue out of your jacket pocket, blow your nose and check your watch. Six minutes will have passed. It should take between five and ten.

You haven't asked, you'll say, how I know that you and Frances slept together.

This will surprise him.

I thought . . . Well, it was obvious in the pub, wasn't it?

But his hand will drop from the door.

Look, you won't like this, but there's something else I need to say. It's a confession really. A while ago, as I said, I was getting worried about her behaviour. I didn't know what else to do.

Do what? What did you do?

I installed bugs around her house.

You what? What do you mean bugs?

Recording devices, and transmitters. Audio and video. I hid them in several places. They're still there. It feels like my house really, so it wasn't a big deal, but I thought I ought to tell you.

Bullshit.

It's true. Do you want to hear?

No.

But you'll produce your phone and press play and he'll have to listen.

Them in the hall. Dull thumps.

I think that's Frances going round the house, you'll say.

My housemate. I wasn't sure if she'd be in.

It'll be like her voice burns him, the way he starts.

This bit's quiet, you'll say. Listen carefully.

I live alone.

You'll return to the centre of the room and he'll retake his place on the sofa. Sighs and gasps will come from your phone, some of them his.

What is this? Why do you have this? Get out.

Will this sound slurred? Your reply will be,

Just listen.

There'll be a rustle and a soft smack.

That was either her bag or your jacket, I think. It sounds heavy, like leather.

You'll point to his jacket hanging behind the door.

His eyes will close. He'll lean back, but remain upright.

Patrick?

The hissing of fabrics. The clicking of buttons. His breath and hers.

You press pause.

Patrick?

You feel required to act surprised. You are surprised.

Patrick? Are you OK?

He is leaning, and the lean moves, then he's floorbound. His head strikes the armrest on the way down.

Patrick?

He lies supine, one knee up, the foot caught under the sofa. You tap his chin. You tap it harder. He is breathing gently. You slide his feet together and fizz the ankles tight with a cable tie. You add another. Feeling bold, you remove his watch and bind his wrists behind his back. You push the armchair to the edge of the room and drag him to the middle. The joined shaft of his legs you lift and use like a tiller to steer him into place. You tape his mouth shut. You hold the back of his head while the roll sings around his beard just getting the earlobes. You add vertical loops like thick helmet straps to restrain the jaw.

You look at him trussed there. You can't believe it. But you don't know how much time you have, so on go your gloves. Out come your wipes. You try to remember all the things you've touched around the flat and get them clean. There haven't been many things, you don't think, but you clean some three times. You're very thorough about the mug-washing especially. In the end you put both mugs aside to throw away.

He hasn't moved. You put the door on the latch and go out to collect your things, wiping the bell button on your return. Still he breathes. You pull on overalls and shoe covers and a cap and a mask, which for now you let hang around your throat. Everything except the shoe covers is white. They are blue. You look like a collector of evidence or a hero in a contaminated zone.

You decide to add more bindings to the wrists and ankles. Afterwards you rope them together into a hogtie, leaving him at the side of the room in the recovery position, more or less. He is very heavy. You push the rest of the furniture and boxes against the walls to make an area of about four square metres where you lay your tarpaulin. It is too large for the space, so you drape it over the furniture and fold it along the edges, a noisy task. This done, you drag Patrick back to the centre, and arrange your tools on the crackling ground. You just have to tolerate the heat inside your overalls.

In the shower you fill the parasol stand with water, but this makes it too heavy to carry, so you empty some out and heave it back into the lounge. There you refill it in instalments with his kettle. You think you hear a groan, and freeze. There is no more. You tie his ankle ligatures to the stand with rope, your fingers quickening. In his pockets you find his keys and phone. You sit with him, thinking about Frances.

His eyes open. He looks at you, and at your tools. You say,

Hi Patrick. I put something in your tea which made you sleep. When you're ready, please nod to show you understand me. Your mouth is taped shut.

What you think is him beginning to nod is in fact him retching. You only understand when vomit comes through his nose, at which you leap forwards and try to lift him to a sitting position so that he can swallow, all while he flexes every which way like a hooked fish. You can't pull the tape off his mouth because you've put so much on, and he'd certainly scream, if only from the pain of his beard being torn out. It might also be hard to put the tape back, so close to the teeth. Nor do you want vomit everywhere. So you just hold him. It's hard work, but he slowly settles. He snorts loudly to clear his nose. You do your best to wipe him clean. You also change your overalls, which have become torn.

Patrick, you say. Hey Patrick. It's OK. Calm down. You'll probably feel quite strange for a few minutes, but it will pass. Take a moment. Hey, listen. *Listen!* Your wrists and ankles are bound with plastic cable ties. You won't be able to break free, but if you struggle they will hurt.

He struggles anyway. Only experience subdues him. No doubt you'd be the same. You let him settle again.

OK. I need the code to your phone. Using your fingers, please show me the first digit. If it's zero, show me ten fingers.

He hesitates then complies, and it is zero.

Thank you. Now the second digit. Great. Now the third. And the fourth.

He's shown you *oooo*. It is not the code.

OK Patrick. I understand that you don't want to cooperate with me, but you need to think about yourself as well. I'm not going to make threats, I just want you to think about the situation you're in, and what my options are if I don't get the correct answer next time. Nod when you're ready to be serious. I'm in no hurry. Good. Now what's the code?

This time his phone responds. You look through the apps he's used most recently. You check his diary and find nothing alarming.

Thanks, you say when you're done.

He's trying to talk, trying to be calm, but his eyes rush round like mice.

I'd like to hear what you have to say, but I can't take off the tape because you'll scream. If you're patient, I'll give you the opportunity later to write something down.

You sip some water from a glass you found.

So I imagine you want to know why I'm dressed like this, and what this stuff is for.

He stares.

Are you religious?

He hesitates. Shakes his head. Shrugs.

Not sure? I think that's fair. I'm not a believer myself, and it leaves me stuck with a lot of questions. When we met we didn't get the chance to talk, but I'd been watching you for a while and you struck me as someone unconcerned by the difficult parts of being. I won't say that you are unreflective. I don't know you yet. You just seemed so sure of yourself, more than a thoughtful person ought to be. Anyway, I thought about you afterwards, and all the things I wished I'd been able to say. There's that wonderful French expression, *esprit d'escalier*, or staircase wit, which describes the frustration of hitting on the perfect remark when it's too late to say it, and I suppose this was a version of that, in a way. I imagined being able to ask you some of the questions that beset me, thinking that to you they would be fresh and troubling. Of course I might be wrong there. Another thing I wanted to know was whether I'd imagined you correctly.

You are hot and breathing heavily. You drink more water and walk unsteadily to the armchair, your plastic shoe covers sliding on the plastic sheet.

Have you ever noticed, you say, lowering yourself into the seat, how our language conflates mystery with greatness? When we want to describe the very best or greatest things of all we don't say *excellent*, which feels weak, or *optimal*, which only engineers say. We say *amazing* or *incredible* or *wonderful* or *fabulous* or *astonishing* or *fantastic*, all words, you'll notice, that mean *inexplicable* or *surprising* or *impossible* or *seemingly untrue*. In order to evoke greatness we evoke our own failure to understand, our ecstasy of interest, the curiosity we feel about how anything so great could come to be. It's funny how much our daily speech reveals without our noticing. *Die Sprache spricht*, as Heidegger said, which means *language talks*, once it's translated.

A lorry rumbles past and the daylight dims.

Now ask yourself whether this works the other way around. When we encounter something inexplicable, do we *ipso facto* call it great? The answer is yes, but that hardly delivers the scale of affirmation needed. Worshipping the presumed greatness of the inexplicable is not just something people do. It's the main strand of human history. The plagues that freed the Israelites, the miracles of Jesus, the early Muslim conquests against impossible odds. God, the greatest thing of all, must be the author of these events, the rationale goes, because they cannot be explained in any other way. God is our absent explanations, and as such He is visible only to us, the one species that seeks them. Eastern religions arrive at the same place by a different route, preaching that people should try to free themselves of all desires, including curiosity, which is the desire to know. In short they solve the quintessential human problem by disinventing our humanity. Samsara, the cycle of rebirth, even presents being alive quite bluntly as a problem that needs solving, and in the process cunningly clouds our fear of death by making immortality a predicament. Who would not wish to achieve acceptance of such a consoling fiction in preference to the fact that we are trapped in a race to understand our lives before they end, and that we cannot win?

He just lies there.

Anyway.

You feed another length of rope through the crook of his left elbow and knot the ends behind a sofa leg. Looking at how you've rigged it, and given that the wrists will separate eventually, you decide it's best to separate them now, so you make a bracelet around the right wrist with your last cable tie and strap this tight to the ankles with more rope. Next you sever the bindings that joined the wrists together, upon which the left springs free and begins to jerk about, making the sofa jolt and simmer. Quickly you take hold of the rope round the elbow and pull the whole arm back until no slack is left for it to move in. This is not difficult to do. Two of your arms are stronger than one of his, and the angle is in your favour, but in order to tie a new knot to secure the arm you end up having to sit on his shoulder, and are fairly bounced about until you're done. At last you stand back to watch. Channels of sweat run down the inside of your overalls. The forearm stiffens and swings, but he does look well trussed. You should have set this up earlier, but it's been useful to test yourself against his strength and the struggle has primed your feelings.

I'm going to cut this off, you say, tapping his left hand. You're right-handed, yes?

He's gone quiet and still.

When I'm finished, I'm going to give you pen and paper, and I'd like you to write down whatever you like. It could be how you're feeling, what you think of me, a confession, anything you want to say. Anything at all.

Now he's nodding crazily. He seems to switch moods fast.

Yes? You will write something?

He nods and nods and nods. He juts his head towards my bag.

You want to write it now?

His eyes are like upturned bowls.

Will you be quick?

The nods are frenzied.

OK. OK. Try this.

You slide the notebook under his right hand, which grabs it like a raft. You put a pen between the fingers, and immediately they begin to write, but being behind his back, and being restricted by the cable ties, the letters merge into a heap of scribble.

Hold it, hold it, you say. I can't read that. Let's start again.

You tear out the page and give the pad back to him.

Write one word, OK? Then tap the pad when you're done.

The fingers resume. They're making a long word from capital letters.

BROTHER? you ask.

He nods and nods. You tear off the page. The next word is shorter and clearer.

COME

Then,

12

BROTHER COME 12?

He's murmuring and jerking around.

You mean you have a brother and he's coming here at twelve?

He taps the pen frantically, almost in triumph. You put the pad back under to protect the tarpaulin. He starts writing again.

HAS, then, *KEY*

You're saying that your brother is going to arrive here at twelve and that he has a key?

He slaps the pen down on its side.

Your watch says 11.32.

What's your brother's name?

His fingers stumble around, knocking the pen out of reach. You pick it up and return it to them. They write,

STEVE

You consult his phone and soon find a strand of recent text messages from *Stevo*. There's stuff about football, and about a university degree. They sound like brothers or very close friends, the way they talk. It's the coarseness and the mockery. Scrolling back further you find mention of *my baby brother*, which appears to mean Patrick. There is nothing about visiting. You search for *Stevo*, *Stephen*, *Steven* and *Steve* in his email. You search his diary and his social media accounts. At last you say,

I think you're lying.

He thrashes around, to the extent that he can. He tries to stab you with the pen as you take it from him.

Listen. Listen to me, Patrick. Even if I believed you, what would I do?

He starts nodding again. Nodding and nodding.

No, forget all that, you say preparing a tourniquet. I've thought about this.

He is trembling.

This is something we are going to share. We are explorers, whether or not we want to be. We both want to know how this is going to feel.

You pull up the mask. A dark expansion fills his jeans.

It won't take long.

He struggles, but the arm is easy to hold. The laws of leverage are with you. You realise that you need a hard surface to lean against, however. You look around for a tray, a large book, anything. The laptop you decide would be too slippery. At last you find a breadboard in the kitchen. There are dull roars when he sees you with it. You unbutton his shirt sleeve and roll it to the elbow, where the rope makes you stop. You loop on the tourniquet, take a deep breath and look at the wrist, nearly the same flecked wheaty brown as the board it's pressed to. There's a covering of golden hair and a pale band where the watch was. Do you begin here? Between the carpal bones and the top of the ulna? There are smudgy little cuts already where he's wriggled against the bindings, and the nobble at the top of the ulna might be useful as a guide. Or do you go in the soft underside? Where the skin is milky and hairless, where the blood is. You're wishing this dilemma on yourself. You should just start without delay.

One of your knees holds down the arm, the other the hand, exposing the wrist between them. Your expensive boning knife is factory sharp and easily parts the skin, but strikes bone straight away beneath it. You'll make no progress with a level blade so you raise the handle and with the point start looking for ligaments. There's little blood at first. It just rises, brims, and rolls neatly to the side. Soon the flow thickens, however. Then you must have hit something because it really starts to go. Now you're digging against a spout. You become impatient. You lift your knee off the wriggling fingers and reach for a roll of plastic sacks. This you slide under the forearm before pressing the hand down on to the board, now slick with blood, hoping to create an angle that will widen the wound. It makes little difference. As you search for better access, his fingers manage to grasp yours, nearly taking the glove off, but he's lost strength and the blood makes everything slippery and you pull free. He's going bananas. You're thankful for the rigging. You turn the arm over and try the soft side. Blood everywhere. You've severed the skin all the way round now, so you try wrenching upwards, hoping to tear the fibres you can't cut. You can't use the mallet and chisel because you need a hand as well as your knees to make the arm lie still. All you have left is the saws. If this is getting done, it's getting done with savagery. The spurts are rhythmic. The blood goes spurt-spurt-spurt, which means you've got an artery, which you expected, but you hadn't expected it to be like this. Perhaps you were too gentle with the tourniquet. At any rate you're glad you have the mask. You read somewhere that surgeons use them not to protect their patients but to shield their own mouths from jets of blood. The bank of towels that you put down is crimsoning.

A last thrust with the saw delivers the hand. You find a dry bit of towel and wipe it reasonably clean. The rest is barely still an arm, all sticks and skin rags. You have the blowtorch to cauterise the stump, but it's difficult to say that there is a stump now. And still the blood and the blood and how it comes. You show Patrick the hand, much heavier to hold than they feel attached. He isn't interested. He's pale. He may be in shock. Treatment at this stage could restore him, or it could squander what time remains. You offer him the pad and the pen again, say something limp, but he just stares. You feel foolish, you with your fancies. You tell him, still out of breath, that if he, writes something he might, stop you, or you're not, going to stop. From nowhere the comforting words of Epicurus come to you, and you remind him of them. *Whatever causes no distress when it is present, gives pain to no purpose when it is anticipated.* All he does is bleed.

Then it's like he knows, like he's been listening, the way he rears up crablike on his head and heels and, you think, tries screaming. There's something past terror in those eyes and cheeks. It's an insisting flash of life, maybe a response to you picking up your chisel, maybe what made you pick it up. Whatever. You get in there, into the soft section of him, into his lifted middle, which gives back to you a kind of *slock slock slock*, all thick and easy. The wing arm flails but it has no hand. Maybe you shout things. Maybe you're too focused. Sometimes you hear a *dink* as you clip a button, and soon his shirtfront's worked to shreds, the gut to slush inside a bowl of bone. You move to tauter areas, such as the thighs and throat. Soon you're exhausted. Don't be surprised by that. In the giddy prison of the moment you'll get carried away but when you pause you will be aching. The chisel handle will be sticking to your fingers. Beneath the glove you'll feel blisters on the rise. You'll think about checking for a pulse but stop when you step back and see what lies in front of you. A red oblong. A Rothko drying. Two blue denim legs then . . . Well, it isn't going to have a pulse. Crouching, you'll knock against the parasol stand

and hear the water lollop. The clean trainers still attached to it will rock along. You'll see that the hand has somehow fetched up among the purplish rubble of the abdomen, beside an almost pristine kidney which you'll cut free and weigh in your palm, letting it slide over your fingers, its tuft of vessels shivering. It will be this sight and the great heat of everything, the wrist-deep warmth, that you'll remember best. The air will be a miasma of rust and dung. Your overalls will start to stick together. You'll become aware of traffic on the road again.

At this point take care not to underestimate the importance, the difficulty or the duration of the cleaning phase, however unrewarding you may find it. Your job, in plain terms, will be to get the body jointed, bagged and hidden, the flat clean, and everything you've used removed from it and burned or otherwise disposed of. You'll not be able to get beyond the detection of forensic science, but remember that forensic scientists find nothing where they don't look. So be finicky. Temporarily disturb yourself with such a pathological meticulousness that even the existence of a crime will stay in dispute. In short, bore the police.

Begin with the body. Seven big cuts make a cadaver manageable. At the knees, hips, neck and shoulders. The head, still bound, still bearded, you'll be able to detach with just a stout knife or cleaver, clearing away the pipes around the vertebrae before splitting them apart with a mallet behind the blade. You will need the saw for the others. That lesson's learned. Don't start getting the idea that you're an artisan. Rigor mortis sets in fast, perhaps before two hours, after which everything becomes more difficult. With the cuts made, put each piece in a waste sack of its own, folding the arms at the elbow and tying them shut. Each sack then goes inside another, but do not on any account be tempted to overfill them. When the time comes to take everything outside you'll want nothing that needs heaving or which might split.

A word on methods. A large male body contains around six litres of blood so the tarpaulin will now look like an abattoir floor, and you a slaughterman. Your main task will be to avoid treading blood around. Once the body parts are bagged replace your overalls. Check that the bags are clean then pile them by the door. If a bag is not clean, put it inside another one. Replace your gloves as often as you need to. The aim is to designate clean and dirty areas and change clothing each time you move from the second to the first, and to do this seldom. You'll be helped by the fact that much of the blood will by now have coagulated into lengths of gel that can be scooped into a bucket. The rest should be mopped up with paper or cotton towels. Bag all loose rubbish. Clear away your tools into their box, and bag that too, along with the breadboard, water glass and mugs. You should now have just a filthy tarpaulin with a parasol stand on top of it. With a sponge and a bucket of water, carefully soak up and rinse out the blood and tissue from them both, starting at the edge of the tarpaulin and working inwards to the middle, folding as you go. Lift the clean parasol stand on to a new refuse sack or spare overall and drag it to the bathroom for emptying. Afterwards wrap it in the tarpaulin and bag them both.

It will have been on your mind that you may have punctured the tarpaulin at some point, and in one place you'll find you have, and that a good quantity of blood has seeped into the carpet. Most homes contain some of the blood of their occupants, but there'll be about a wineglassful down there, nearly a foot outside the edge of the rug. The carpet will be one of those coarse hard-wearing ones common in rented property and too tightly woven to clean. If you move it to cover the stain, the rug will look strangely placed, and invite investigation. Fetching a knife from the bags you'll therefore try to cut the stain away. The blade will flex awkwardly under the pressure you have to apply, but soon you will have the red section removed, leaving a ragged D-shaped hole. This will look strange too, or at least like it needs explaining, until you hit upon the idea of singeing the edges with the blowtorch. Now it will look as though Patrick deliberately placed the rug strangely in order to conceal an accident of his own, most likely with one of his cigarettes. Lastly you'll go round rearranging and spraying everything, the leg of the sofa about four times.

When the flat is clean, bag your things and his jacket. The wallet from it you'll leave in a line on the kitchen counter with the watch, phone and keys. Then you'll change your mind and bag them all, dismantling the phone. Before opening the door, sit down. Slow your breathing. Try to imagine being a detective arriving here. It will occur to you that the extent of your cleaning may itself raise suspicions, so you'll fetch pillows from the bed and shake them wherever you've cleaned in the hope of dusting any sterile patches with his sheddings. You may be aware that you are delaying again. It's carrying out fifteen bags that you'll be dreading.

Deep breaths again. Deep breaths and busy but unhurried walking will get it done. You will be seen, but it's not about whether you will be seen, it's about whether you are remembered. You will have been skittish about looking for cameras, not wanting to stare into one, but you'll not think there are any. You'll remove your overalls and tuck them into a bag. You'll tell yourself that you've done well and open the door to air, driving, chirrups, cumulus, growth, urban planning, conservation, conversation, wavelengths, architecture, shade, idiolects, signage, particulates, law, fashion, accessibility provision, isobars, handlebars, residents' parking. You'll flinch from the rushing river of it, you on the bank, knowing that to those afloat the river is all. You'll put the bags out on the concrete and shuttle to your van eight times. The loading of vans is mundane. You'll be a paragon of the nondescript.

You'll pull away into the afternoon, a late Saturday afternoon, and in the sun the warmest of the week. On the way home you'll pass through those sections of the city where the young convene, skin for placards, declaring independence. All day you'll have had your homecoming in mind, promising yourself that you will rest and let the street grow dark before bringing in the bags, but when the homecoming comes you'll sway so with fatigue that any rest you begin will close the day, so you'll pack the entire load into your chest freezer immediately, following which you'll shower. You'll make no notes. You'll leave that for the morning, many black hours distant. You'll put yourself to bed. You'll lie on your side, the smell still in your nostrils, remembering.

SHE RISES WELL TODAY, WITH PLANS. She runs. Afterwards she takes down her neglected recipe books, makes notes and sighs at the photographs. They talk like it's so easy. She buys what she needs and cooks timidly with music on.

Steph rings. She and Greg and some friends, nice people, are going for drinks in the evening at a place that has just opened. Would Frances like to come? To celebrate? Just a small Sunday thing. The voice is soft, the phrases kindly, but it all smells of afterthought. Frances says she's busy and feigns regret.

Dinner is roasted vegetable couscous with pomegranate jewels and a chilli and mint dressing. It was easy. Her plate clean, the counters cleared, she takes her laptop into the front room and places ads for a new housemate. She reads the internet in bed, the machine wheezing. Tomorrow she will book someone to mend the bathroom fan.

Monday morning she runs early, before the day. When the owner opens the cafe, Frances is already in position, pacing. Coffee for breakfast. For lunch a jacket potato with tuna and sweetcorn. The man does not come.

Tuesday she runs a mile more. She could have done two more miles. When she has finished her cheese sandwich, the cafe owner asks what this is really about. Frances says again that she is waiting for a man. The owner's name is Dawn. This is announced like a secret once Dawn has folded herself into a seat at the same table. (They are her seats and her tables, after all.) Frances describes the day she cried and met the well-dressed man. Dawn says she remembers, vaguely. She doesn't sound sure.

He has my phone number, but I don't have his. He said he comes here a lot. Are you certain you don't know him?

Sorry. Doesn't sound like one of my regulars. But I'm not the best with faces.

Do you think you would recognise him if he came back?

Dawn considers this.

I might, she says. But I might not. You must be so bored in here all day! How long do you plan on sticking to it?

I'm not bored. I have my book. There's nothing else I have to do.

The running persists in Wednesday's rain. Back in the warm house, Frances drags the clips from her hair and leaves them in a puddle by the sink. Briefly she becomes emotional. She loves this place, right down to the air inside.

Hooking the door to the wall, Dawn greets her with a special *Mor-ning* that rises and falls in even halves. It means *You belong in my day now,* but you can't just say that to people or you'll frighten them. On the other hand Dawn can't say nothing. It is unusual for someone to spend five consecutive working days waiting in a cafe, so if she does not share her feelings it suggests her feelings need to be concealed. *Nice to see you again* would be the easy choice, but that also makes it the most likely way to lie. Saying *Morning* as she did, making a weary recitation of it, like a class of schoolchildren, superficially says that Dawn is getting tired of seeing Frances every day. If this were true, however, she would hide it, so Frances knows that it is probably a joke meaning the opposite, and the irony requires Frances to imagine Dawn's real feelings, which involves imagining her mind, a moment of actual friendly contact rather than a plain statement that their friendship exists. That's unless Dawn is double-bluffing. Some people do hide behind self-parody. Frances has vegetable lasagne for lunch and the man does not come.

She wonders if he might be away on business. She wonders if writers go away on business, and if he really is a writer. She knows that there are literary festivals and book tours, and that there is research. He might be having a really fertile spell. He might be housebound. A frenzy of coffee and takeaways and typing and milestones toasted with good wine, all the squalid glamour of it. His desk will be a cemetery of cups, his computer a solid servant of many years to which he'll deny being superstitiously attached like a child to his stiffening blanket. He will admit other rituals, like starting early. He dips his pen in dew. No. Delete that. Starting late. He'll be a dark one, a typist of the night, a fierce mechanism while others sleep, and sleeping now. There'll be long lulls grimacingly borne, maybe whole days still-handed, then the breakthrough. Ideas tear out of him like oil bursting a wellhead. There'd be no thoughts of cafes at these times.

The letter sacking her arrives Thursday. It hisses across the mat when she opens the door after her run. It's unexpected, but only in the sense that she's not had expectations. Work has receded in her mind that much. She reads the termination agreement several times, and in the end understands that they are offering to pay her two and a half times her annual salary to leave the company and never discuss why. A confidentiality clause of this kind is normal, but the figure is outlandish. Usually when constructively dismissing someone the tactic is to offer an insultingly low settlement, await angry rejection, then pretend to cave in by making a better offer, which is then usually snatched like victory. This offer looks desperate. *Thirty months' salary at the rate stipulated in the Employee's contract of employment.* She can't find any ambiguity there. She checks her contract of employment and it stipulates what it should. She wonders whether the figure in the termination agreement could be a mistake. She wonders whether this is what she is supposed to wonder, whether she is meant to want to sign immediately before the mistake is found. *We want this done today*, is what this says to her. She signs and showers.

She watches a bald man at the table two away from her. He's a lawyer maybe, with his papers. She watches him scribble, then a phone call brings good news. He gives a little *Yes!* like a child winning. You can see he's desperate to tell somebody what has happened from the way he wriggles on the flat of his seat. He's embarrassed but in the end he turns to her, as she knew he would.

I don't even need this now, he says laughing, indicating his many documents.

She smiles but says nothing, curious to see if he will continue unencouraged.

It's a patent application. Not mine, he adds quickly, almost insulted by himself. Mine's granted. These guys were trying to rip me off.

What's the product?

Spray-on insulation. For pipes, for baths, for walls . . . there's loads of uses. Much better than the normal stuff. It'll cut people's U-values by thirty per cent at least. More if it's an old house. Twelve years I've put into this.

The rest she doesn't listen to. He seems to have nobody to phone.

Late on Friday Dawn asks Frances gently about her plans for the weekend. The man does have her number, remember. If he wants to, he can call.

Honestly, I don't mind waiting, Frances says. If that's OK with you?

It's fine.

In fact, she has some young concerns. She's begun remembering the man's brusqueness at their meeting in the pub. Like maybe he was in a hurry to get away, or not good in crowds. He might have presumed things, seeing her and Patrick. The men had been tense together. He might remember her drunk.

She could always try the pub again. Dawn is right. It is the weekend. The police did not ban her from the place, and she won't interfere. Then with the thought formed it's just the easiest thing to let it push her there, and almost into me.

But that's habits for you, as I've said before. Get too accustomed to your subject's habits and in the end it trips you. I was tired. I had stopped expecting Frances to go anywhere but the station after a day in the cafe. My mind had wandered. I don't remember where. She must have been heading straight towards me for some time before I fled.

I'd not imagined this book as a kind of treatise but it seems to have become one, and there's an honesty in letting it become what it wants. I am trying to be honest. Really that's all I'm trying to be. I began because I had accumulated all these notes and they were clamouring to be heard. And keeping secrets, that makes a clamour too. Plus of course I'd been saying I was a writer for years, when asked. As a result I've had to talk about the practice a fair amount and imagine what it's like. It's not like I imagined.

They were so timid, my first attempts. Like a farmer planting seed in new land, I had a sense of how things might go with lucky weather but no confidence about my guesses. I was slow. I wanted to get it right and I agonised over everything and deleted everything. I could have written an assured paragraph of commentary on each word I chose, then a well-structured chapter about that paragraph, then a charming memoir about this crazy chapter. What do you do when there are more choices than time to choose? It worried me.

Patrick's van was the turning point, I think. Fifteen times I passed it on the way to and from my own, a bag in each hand. I appraised the detritus on the dashboard. I imagined the boxes inside and wondered whether I should have used boxes myself, perhaps with a trolley. I became mindful of the fact that I might want to tell you about these things in the book or journal that by then I had a pretty firm intention of writing. Therefore on each pass I began gathering other observations, on the van's condition, on its type, on its parking style. It was a tether for my restive mind. Then on perhaps the sixth or seventh pass a thought occurred to me. In order to describe this experience honestly I would now have to tell you that I'd been preoccupied at the time by trying to observe things worth describing. Instinctively I was reluctant to admit this, since it suggested that my actions, even accurately recorded, had themselves been steered by thoughts of telling you about them, and as such my life itself had become a kind of fiction. Directly afterwards, of course, I realised that I could not be completely honest unless I also told you about my dilemma about what to tell you. And about that dilemma too. I'd have to admit that this was in my mind while the blood-bellied sacks were in my hands. Henceforth merely intending to write about my experiences would cause me to live at a remove from them, I realised. Just considering myself a writer had put the rest of me on a stage where I would stay until the book was finished. This clinched the decision to complete the first page the following day. I would be rough with it, if necessary.

Since then the urge to write has grown, and recently been overwhelming. Like that farmer again, I face the harvest no longer worried about having enough but about having enough time. These nights have been rich black loam for me, for all the inconvenience involved and the discomfort lately. I'd been sleeping and writing in my van quite a bit, so last week I set up new quarters. I don't like being at home any more. Plus I was losing a lot of time driving hither and yon when I needed to be close to Frances. The new quarters are dark and cramped, and I'm invariably tired when I arrive, but I wake my machine, and idly read yesterday's pages, and my fingers are drawn in. Soon I'm going at it without let-up, forlornly excited, knowing I can't get everything down, knowing how much I'm losing, determined to get all I can. I also know I'm given to expatiating, so forgive me for that. As things wind down I can feel myself being a Penelope or a Scheherazade about this story, creeping back in to spin it out, and spin it out. At the same time I am the ambitious suitors, and the bloodthirsty king.

Every day for hours she sat in the cafe while I watched and listened through suitable devices. Looking back at the early notes now they are so redolent of the time that it makes me hear again the claps of crockery and the swish of the coffee machine, glad yet fretful sounds. Because these were ragged days, the light hours gazing in wonder at her devotion, the nights with body parts to hide.

I had thought vaguely of a country burial, but the more I considered the plan the less I liked it. Even setting aside technique, stray rocks or roots, and how conspicuous you leave the earth, the digging would not be easy. A grave has to be more than a metre deep, more like two ideally, or else burrowing animals take an interest. That's why you hear so much about shallow graves. You don't hear anything about the deep. Two metres down then, and about one square. Could I dig that, then fill it, quietly and in the dark by hand? If I could it would take three nights, I estimated, between which my unfinished work would spend two daytimes on display. I could rent a remote cottage and dig in the grounds, but that would leave clear proof should investigators one day take an interest in me.

Further ideas came. I could attempt to dissolve the body in acid, though that makes fumes and needs equipment. I could buy a boat and drop it at sea, each piece weighted against the buoyancy of its decomposition gases. I could acquire land and build something with concrete foundations. They might have been good ideas, but they were no good for me. I was in strange shape, though I was working on it. Those guys they catch, you know, those guys they catch with segments in the freezer – a sign infallible of nutty murdering, it's said – those guys were working on it too. A freezer is what you have until you have a plan. And even as Sunday and Monday passed, then other days, that Saturday stayed frozen. In truth I was reluctant to go back to the bags at all. I just wanted them gone quickly. I began to find reasons to stay away from home, in the van at first. Then I tried a hotel, but I didn't like being seen coming and going, or having people clean my room. Nor was I keen on the paperwork of renting.

I'm not about to announce an easy answer, by the way. As far as I'm aware there isn't one, which is why there's such ingenuity in the literature. While researching gravedigging however, I did get to know some graveyards, and in the end my answer came from there. Graves are generally dug a few days before the funerals that need them. Time it carefully, therefore, and I might be able to dig a shallow grave in the bottom of a deep one, then let the subsequent ceremony finish things on my behalf. Privacy would not be difficult to find, not if I worked at night, when graveyards are reliably deserted by all but a few intrepid hobos. The difficult thing, it turned out, was finding graves. People don't get buried with the regularity they used to. We're less particular about our condition in the afterlife, and besides there isn't space. Really the only exceptions are the wealthy and religious. Increasing the difficulty was the fact that I couldn't exactly bring the bags along each night while I searched for a plot. If I found one I'd have to go back, empty the freezer, then return in order to begin what I guessed would amount to three hours' digging. I could not overrun into the morning under any circumstances. In effect this restricted me to the four nearest graveyards, with time to search no more than two per night. The best turnover was at a large Muslim cemetery, but that was almost an hour's drive. Each night therefore I toured the nearer grounds and came home defeated, for at most a couple of hours' sleep. Sometimes I took modafinil, which is an excellent wakefulness-promoting drug used by pilots, students and narcoleptics. You'll find it online. Even so I was tired and edgy.

Now Patrick was on the internet. Always the same photograph of him in some bar, pink from holidaying. It did the rounds beside accurate descriptions of his final days and a big *MISSING*. Frances was too busy to see it. Every morning she returned to the cafe, never late. Sometimes I'd nod off in my van and she'd be the first thing I saw on waking. She'd read or eat, or gaze through the window. Sometimes she wrote things down in a black notebook. I don't know whether anything in my life has made me happier. The memory of her dedication and patience drove me on at night as I climbed wet railings, slipped down mudslopes, contemplated pits. Sometimes when the cafe was about to close I'd leave the van and find a discreet place to stand where I could watch her in the flesh.

Even so, I grew disconsolate. I've been persistent enough with projects in the past. I have that kind of character. But the repeated failure to find a grave was getting me down. Probably it was the accumulation of lost sleep or mental strain. Seeing that I could not carry on much longer, I reviewed my plan, and hit upon the idea of reading the death notices at mosques. Muslims bury their dead quickly so they make big announcements, and on Sunday afternoon, when the cafe was closed, I came across a funeral planned for Monday at the large cemetery, which I still had time to scout in daylight. I felt conspicuous among the veiled and bearded mourners at the place but they had their own worries and paid me no attention. With little effort I found the promised grave of Anwar M, a good plot, newly dug, beside a line of bushes. That night under a thin moon and full of modafinil I clambered down. There'd been rain so the ground was soft but sticky. My boots became earthen clubs. With the grave already deep, it was a serious effort to lift each shovelful clear without tipping it on myself. Once the hole deepened, it was impossible. I therefore developed a method of tipping the soil into spare refuse sacks, which by luck I had with me, and storing these up on the grass. The sacks were too heavy and loose to lift above my head, so I had to tie each one to the shaft of my shovel, climb out, then heave it upwards, before lowering myself back in. Even with my spare shovel propped up as a step, the climbing was hard. A couple of times I thought I wouldn't manage it. The method made progress though, and I could count the bags to judge how much, which helped with morale. Even so the first hints of sun appeared while I was still down there, forcing me to remove my night goggles, which I trod into the earth. Twenty bags was my target. Three more to go. When I hauled myself out of the grave for the last time I was shaking. I dropped in all my tools along with the frozen sacks, the hard forms inside already softening at the edges. The soil went on top, giving at least a thirty-centimetre covering, I reckoned, with a small surplus that I dumped on the gravedigger's own pile. At nearly six I trudged away, my hands raw and my back aching. I slept until eleven. On waking, I returned, and in the light drizzle watched the funeral of Anwar M from a nearby grave, feigning grief with real tears.

—

Look, basically all I'm saying is that I'm aware I am bound to have an effect on you that is sometimes the effect I mean, sometimes another effect, usually not even an effect I know about, and that therefore, whatever my meaning, I will generally fail to communicate it, and you will likewise almost certainly fail to understand, having your own limitations as I have mine, but that we should nevertheless try, and keep trying, because eventually the paths of our failures will cross out everything that isn't who we are.

She saw me of course but didn't expect to, not there and then, so it is only now as she waits at the bar that she begins wondering. Was it me? Did I see her? Did I flee? She runs back out and peers through the slots in the crowd. All week she's been imagining my face at the cafe door, her calmness in triumph, Dawn's smiles on the back of her neck. Is it instead going to be a jab on my shoulder at the hot end of a chase through rush hour? She returns to the bar. She stews. She wonders if she has regrets, and the next day tells Dawn.

That's good news! Cheer up! It means he's still around.

I suppose, she says.

Her doubts widen as Saturday draws on but she sticks with it and in the evening goes back to the pub, where the walls are for some reason draped with bunting, and the next evening too. The pub is one room like the cafe but so large and at times so busy that I could easily go unseen. Plus she is accosted almost hourly.

Whoever stood you up's a fucking plonker, said a small man in late middle age and a little drunk, his head stuck out of a group then quickly pulled back in. He would be married, she supposed, and this his chaste revival of the old days, like the maintenance of a motorbike that stays in the shed. *Whoever stood you up's a fucking plonker.* It was the phrasing that made her smile, the junction between its gallant front and muddy rear.

You're with Frayne Peters, right? Third floor? That was a young guy. He offered his hand smartly and she shook it without thinking. *I'm in M&A,* he said into her eyes.

And in his early twenties she guessed. The doubt concerned whether he was a teenager. He had that adolescent formality, like a boy playing a man with only movies to go on. It would be charming for as long as it was inept. She gave him, *I'm sorry. You've got me confused with someone else.* And a stare.

On Monday she wears a fitness tracker for her run. It says she's gone two and a half miles. On Tuesday she goes four. When she gets home she undresses and lies down, self-vanquished, her blood jumping.

Dawn asks about the notebook for the first time.

Just some thoughts, Frances says.

What about?

Dawn's husband drove taxis, was a character and died. What kind of character Dawn won't say. She's spoken of him with only buried fondness, and that only once, giving the bare facts of an immaculate smoker's death of lung cancer at the age of forty-eight following a five-month cough, three stunned weeks from diagnosis to demise. There'd been insurance. She said it felt as though some magic spell had turned her husband into money. Mick his name was. There'd not been time to find out how it felt to him. So anyway, in fear of frittering, Dawn's riches went on an old friend's cafe and the old friend went to Spain. No ceremony marked the change of ownership although the regulars were welcoming to Dawn and some spoke of noticeable improvements, most the result of the new hotplate being clean. Because she wasn't doing this for love, you know. She said so a few times, and the hard words carried easily from the delivery entrance round back, where she stood with a cigarette in her outdoor hand. Why did she do it then? A shrug and a puff. One laugh. *You've got to do something haven't you?* There the matter closed. She would not mention Mick again, and soured if you tried. The smoking was her statement, Frances decided, a defiance of the disease that they could not defeat. She was fifty-four and already had the look of an old woman beset by living.

Oh you know, about people. And some of the things they say.

You mean my customers?

Sometimes.

Two weeks later I rang during the three o'clock slump.

Hi. Is that Frances?

Yes.

She waited, but she knew. She sat still in her seat, like there was danger in sudden movement, then did a slow half-turn and nodded at Dawn, who mimed cheering. I asked if she remembered me and said sorry I'd been slow to call. I had some free time at last, I said. I'd been wondering how things turned out. Would she tell me after work one evening?

Ha! There is no work! she said.

What?

They fired me. Now I'm not allowed to talk about it.

Oh. God, I'm so sorry.

Thank you. It's been a very strange time.

I'm sure. Do you have something new lined up?

I'll be all right.

What happened?

I'm not supposed to say, remember. We can talk about other things when we meet.

Things that *are* allowed?

Yes.

We settled on Friday, then there was one of those pauses.

Actually I was hoping you would ring, she said. There's something else I wanted to ask. That time I saw you in the pub. Sorry, I was a little wasted.

I remember. I mean I remember seeing you. You seemed fine.

Thanks, but I was wasted. Do you remember the guy I was with? The guy who was sitting next to me, I mean.

I didn't answer.

Quite a big guy. I think you talked to him about some job he was doing. He's a delivery driver. I'd never met him before, and I haven't seen him since. I just need to get a message to him but I don't have his details. Do you remember the name of the client on that job you talked about? A publisher, I think. It's a long shot, but I thought I'd ask.

Oh yes. I remember. He did talk about a publisher, didn't he?

I hummed and sighed while I checked my notes.

Matinee Press? Was that it?

Yes! Thank you, I'm sure that's right. Matinee.

She went pink. She was so happy.

I went home to get some things. I say home but it didn't feel that way. I'd not really been able to sleep there since the funeral so I'd been moving my stuff out by degrees and not been back for a week or so. This was yesterday. Already it feels like my real home is here, in my new quarters, cramped as they are.

So I went back to my former home, I should say, and it seemed distant to me. Not less familiar. If anything the familiarity I experienced was more intense because I had to consider it. When you live with things every day you recognise them effortlessly and as a result don't notice yourself doing it. They are ordinary to you. Once things fall out of your daily life, however, recognising them starts to require an act of recollection. A small act, but enough to make you notice and take interest, like first wiping away a coat of dust.

I intended to be quick but I lingered, transfixed by the sight of the old pen jar. Then it was the same over an unwashed cup. It got me thinking that perhaps the most intense interest possible would come from visiting your childhood home and finding everything preserved exactly as it was when you were a child. All the same mess. The same scuffs and accoutrements. You'd look around and everything would be exotic and familiar at once. It would be quite disturbing, I think, because what's ordinary to you is a good map of who you are. You'd see how much you change without noticing. What's ordinary to me now, in my new home, is darkness and this screen, and being as stealthy as I can.

PATRICK'S MISSING. THE PUBLISHERS say so right away. They've spoken to the family a few times. The family have been in touch a few times. The publishers feel so awful for them, they wish they could do more. At last they find the brother's number. He's Steven Lacey with a V. Type *Patrick Lacey* and the screen swarms. The brother has been busy. He's got a website going. It's cheap-looking and misspelled. There's a police investigation number everywhere. When Frances calls they take her details and say they'll call her back. She tries to explain that it's strange, because there's other police already looking for Patrick. Her boss died and the last time she saw Patrick the police were at her house. They say they'll call her back. She calls the first police and gets the DI something who rang her before. He is nice, and confirms that the investigation remains open, but it takes a while for him to recall the case and who she and Patrick are. Even then this news about her alibi fails to stir him. She thought he'd think her brave and honest and was braced for questions. Maybe he thinks Will was suicide. Anyway, he has the name.

She calls Steven Lacey. He sounds busy but pleased. He

asks if they can meet at the mother's home so she takes a train east and follows his directions through a retail park and into a grid of dowdy residential roads. The houses are not long built but already look like they regret it. The gardens are past mowing, or paved and parked on. Rust trails hang down the walls from the boilers' overflows.

She rings the bell and as she waits it starts to rain. A breeze hits the street, mussing up the trees provided. Her finger is ready to ring again when the door opens. Muttering, the mother motions her into a narrow hallway thick with dog. A staircase reaches up the left wall, and on the right a glass door dapples the lounge, where the mother goes. Money has been spent in here, but little recently. The give in the sofa has gone and the grey flanks of an old television jut deep into a carpet that shows the work of paws. The mother takes a chair and points to the sofa. A greasy-looking Yorkshire terrier appears and jumps round ratifying everything.

Steve should be back any minute, the mother says. Can I get you a drink? Tea, coffee, juice?

Her own glass holds something fizzy and clear.

Thank you. Actually I'd love a tea.

Milk and sugar? Get down, Carlos!

Milk no sugar. Thanks.

The mother moves wearily. She is younger than Frances expected and has given good looks to her son. After a long time she returns, collected somewhat by the rhythms of tea-making. She passes the cup through a cloud of perfume.

Thanks. I can't imagine how awful this must be for you. I'm so sorry.

The woman smiles but says nothing. In speaking there are traps.

I'm Frances, by the way.

Steve told me. Lindsey. Pleased to meet you.

They are too far apart to shake hands and it seems not worth standing up, so Frances does a little wave, then regrets the flippancy. It loosens something in Lindsey, however.

Sorry I was slow with the door earlier. It's. It's the not knowing. I understand that something terrible might have happened. You can't not think about it. But even. It sounds bad but even if I did hear the worst, you know, if that phone went now. Or if it hadn't been you at the door. She is looking more at the carpet than at Frances. And people do still phone, you know. Then they talk about your energy bills and you just have to deal with it. I don't know what's normal but I keep thinking there must be something wrong with me because I'm not getting used to it at all. Not at all. For a long time Steve said I shouldn't worry, then we heard that Patrick wasn't showing up for jobs. You think horrible, horrible things. You can't help it. And you can't really say it to people, but if I heard the worst, you know. If the worst happened. I could stop feeling like it was going to happen any moment.

The dog sleeps on her feet, its ears twitching.

What do the police say?

They say they're doing what they can. Steve convinced them to search the flat. They've talked to all his friends. He's registered as a missing person, so we'll know if his credit cards get used. They say when young men disappear it's usually volitional.

Do you know any reason why he might have run away? Is his business in trouble?

Steve's been looking into that. I know it wasn't doing brilliantly, but I thought it was OK. He has a bit of debt. Steve reckons the police will just let the bailiffs find him.

I suppose as long as he's found.

Lindsey's hands encircle the whole glass.

How about Patrick's dad, is . . .

We're divorced.

OK.

But he knows. He's been helping a little on the phone.

The door opens and an even larger version of Patrick appears, maybe with less hair, lacking some of the finer edges. He kisses his mother and tells her he has the posters. Then he gives Frances his attention, and a shake of his hand.

I'm Steven. Thanks so much for coming down.

No one has seen Patrick since the Friday night, when he went drinking with friends. One of them remembers he had a job the next day, and there was a booking in his diary, but the client emailed to cancel on Saturday morning, and his phone was off by lunchtime. The van appears not to have been used. Bringing all this together, Steve's belief is that his brother, finding himself at a loose end, went into the city for personal reasons that morning, using public transport. He left no record of any arrangements, and no footage of him has been found on the buses and trains that were nearby, although not all the footage has been checked. There is too much of it, the companies say. Besides, the weather was good and he might have walked.

There is no reason to imagine that Patrick is involved in anything dangerous or illegal. He takes drugs recreationally but has never sold them, to the best of anybody's knowledge. He is single and appears to have had no regular girlfriend since the end of a long-term relationship last year. That woman, now with someone else, says it's been months since she saw him. No other women had realised he'd gone. If he intended to disappear it must have been an intention quickly formed because the recent documents folder on his computer shows that on Friday afternoon he'd been developing plans to take his business online. That may have been why he went into town, for some kind of research.

Oh my God, that was my idea! We talked about it that night.

Your idea to start the website?

Well, not a website. But I said he should consider a presence in online auctions. That's where people buy things that need delivering. He didn't sound interested, I thought.

Could you tell me everything you can remember about your time together, from the beginning?

She does, and in the telling she remembers more. Some are clean pieces of fact, some just edgeless feelings. The solemnness of that cigarette, but also his wryness in the pub, and afterwards their lust and laughter. She tells it all, daintily where she can, and finds herself describing a young man enjoying life. He did seem to have pleasure to live for. At any rate she knows she thought so at the time. Appearances can, well, we all know what they can do. When she gets to Patrick leaving she feels embarrassed for the first time. Had he given her his real number, had she heard it properly, had she just known his surname, things might have gone another way. She treads carefully lest some fault of hers lies scattered among the facts, and rushes by what happened to Will. She can't deny it's weird. Two men in two weeks. The X where their paths crossed marking her.

Thank you, Steve says. I need to make a couple of phone calls. Can I give you a lift to the station when I'm done? It's chucking down out there.

Thanks, but I'll be fine.

They stand and shake hands. The dog scuttles in to be involved. As Steve's footsteps fade above their heads, Frances makes ready to leave, but Lindsey remains sitting.

I'm so glad you came, she says. It's like I could hear Pat in some of what you said. It's been a while since we heard anything new.

I just wish I could do more. Or that I'd done something different. Maybe he just needs to be alone for a few weeks?

Maybe. There's no other good way to explain it, is there?

Frances feels set the task of trying, but the silence while she thinks becomes her answer.

Steve's been amazing, Lindsey says. He's used up nearly all his annual leave to move back here and run things. I'd be lost otherwise.

He's an amazing brother. I'm sure if anyone could find Patrick.

Frances hops from foot to foot. It feels awkward to be standing, awkward to sit back down.

They're very close. Very close. Sibling rivals, you know, even though Steve's five years older. I think maybe it's been helpful for him to make a project out of this. She actually laughs. I'm just a total mess.

Anybody would be. Frances approaches to place a hand on her back.

Probably. I don't know. She stands. I need a top-up. Can I get you anything? Another tea? There's biscuits if you'd like one?

No thank you. I'm fine.

Frances makes a circuit of the room while Lindsey is in the kitchen. There are reproduction watercolours in matching frames. Here a meek hillside, there a tepid shipwreck. She knows it's garbage but tries to know something else. She feels a kind of fellowship with this stricken family. Like they've each brought their own impression of Patrick and together made a mould, his absence at the centre. Lindsey returns with a tea of her own and says,

I decided to follow your example. I've not met many of Pat's girlfriends. Not that you are his girlfriend. I know that. I just mean he keeps that side of things to himself. Nowadays I suppose people do settle down much later than they used to, and he doesn't want his mum poking her nose in anyway. You don't have kids?

No. No, I don't. I'm not with anyone. Work doesn't leave a lot of time.

She wonders why she is making excuses.

What do you do?

I suppose I'm unemployed.

I'm sorry.

That's OK.

So they talk about lost jobs and in particular the job that

Lindsey loved, working reception in a radiology department, until Lindsey says,

I think I will have that biscuit.

Frances follows her this time into a small, neat kitchen, the walls clad in pine boards, orange and uneven and studded with hooks around the window, from which hang ladle, tongs, whisk, spatula and other utensils. Above the draining board, two more hooks hold photographs of Steven and Patrick as children, the younger proudly freckled, the older narrowly tolerating a maroon uniform. Frances places her cup in the sink, then overrules herself and washes it.

Oh there's no need for that! Lindsey says, pleased.

Prising off the lid of a tin with dogs on it, she offers Frances first pick from a stack of homemade cookies, which engulf them both in warm vanilla.

Those look amazing.

Frances takes a bite and with a squeal lifts her hand to catch the crumbs.

How does this happen? she thinks. How does a woman waiting for news of her son's death conceive the desire to bake cookies? Are they fuel for Steven? Were they made for her visit? The tin is quite full and they are fresh.

These are fantastic, she says. Don't tell me you made them yourself?

Oh it's not difficult. Lots of butter and an egg, a basic soft cookie really. I've been making them for years.

They're really, really good.

Thank you.

They talk about cooking. With effort, the dog pushes through the door to join them. Presently Frances sees it visit what appears to be a litter tray in the corner. When it finishes, Lindsey removes the small crumbed stool with a plastic bag, inverts it, ties the handles, and drops the package into a dustbin in the garden. On her return her cardigan sparkles with raindrops not yet drawn into the wool.

Sorry about that, she says, and it is true that Frances was tardy in hiding her disgust. I think what's hard, what I really struggle with, is that Pat never goes this long without visiting. It's not something I can tell my friends, if I'm being tactful. With some of their children, you know, you'll hear nothing until Christmas. One of them goes missing and you'd believe they had a secret life, but with Pat I can't. I try to. Steve tries to make me. But I can't. I feel like I do know this isn't him. He only moved out two years ago, and he's been back so often. I suppose it's because his dad and me aren't together any more. Maybe he takes pity on me. Or actually. She laughs. Actually it's probably just because I've got his fishing rods.

He likes fishing?

Oh my God. He is obsessed with it! There's a bit of river he goes to just behind these houses. You should see his room. I'll show you.

And what way is there to refuse? So up the narrow stairs they go into the first room on the landing which, as promised, is full of angling magazines and plastic boxes and rods that twitch like whiskers in the stirred air.

Wow.

Some of it he's had since primary school.

It's incredible.

It is. The orderliness, the array, the bellowing of *Carp!* by a thousand covers.

Do you fish as well? Frances says.

You must be joking! That was his dad. Steve enjoyed it for a while, but nothing like Pat.

She steps deeper into the room. Frances wants to go now. She feels a fraud and a failure.

Mum! Steve is calling from next door. That was the bus company. They'll do it.

That's great news, Lindsey says. Oh well done!

It's unsold ad space, Steve explains when they go through to join him. They've agreed to use our poster instead of house ads next month. It's only for the month, but a lot of people will see it.

He swings his chair to face them, full of accomplishment, a spreadsheet on the screen behind him. There are storage boxes on the floor and squares of paper on the walls. They itemise what was found in the flat and make a timeline of Patrick's last known hours. Frances herself is there.

I think it's amazing what you're doing, she says.

Steve shrugs.

You've got to do something. Are you sure you don't want that lift?

She fetches the laundry basket from the cupboard under the stairs and turns on the kitchen lights. The clean clothes have gone cold and stiff in the machine and she hauls them out like a great cable from the sea. Those that can take mechanical drying she puts back, carrying the rest to the boiler cupboard where she droops them over the slats, plus a few leftovers on a radiator, and a few more on another. The smell of tired water mixes with the smell of the chicken stock on the stove, a large batch, simmered from roasted bones. Last time it made a rich and flavoursome risotto, the best she has yet cooked.

She mops the kitchen floor and thinks about Patrick and his family. Being with the brother was hard. It is hard to be with heroes. Driving to the station, he looked only forwards and shared some troubles that he hadn't shared with Lindsey. Patrick's flat is one. The landlord is now owed two months' rent, and has warned them that he will have to advertise for a new tenant and retain the deposit if the next is missed as well. Steve does not think the family can pay, and is worried that evidence may be destroyed when the flat's relet. The police searched it once but rather casually, he thought. There'd not been the tents and space-suits he was expecting. New developments will get them interested, he thinks, but his hopes for some are thinning. People just get bored after a while. The few calls that still come are all wellwishers or gossips. He no longer shows their messages to his mother. Next Wednesday he must return to his job managing a timber yard. He isn't sure, but he thinks he'll quit instead to keep the search going. He reckons they'll rehire him when he's finished. *Mum's just not up to it right now and Dad,* he said, *Dad's not the kind of guy you give important stuff to. Pat would have a right laugh at that.* And he laughed too. Then he said, *Of course everything would be different if it was someone's little girl. Not just my . . .* He couldn't say *little brother*. She saw the work in his eyes. He was hoarding something savage.

She decides to pay Patrick's rent herself, for a month at least. She'll email Steve and insist. He's too practical to be proud. Going upstairs for her laptop, she passes what in her mind is still Steph's room, though it is bare now. The external walls are speckled with black where moisture was allowed to condense behind costume mounds. That'll need dealing with. Her steps echo. *Echo,* the word people call to summon one.

She makes tea and emails Steve in the front room. It takes time to find the right tone, the right firmness that will keep her offer from starting a discussion. She sweeps the grate and lights a new fire. She considers breaking up the remnants of the kitchen chair for wood, but she quite likes the chair. It could be mended. It just looks messy where it is. She gets up to see if it will fit in the loft, but on her way out to the hall she sees something else. She stops. On the floor below the coat hooks, half-hidden by her coats, is a pair of men's shoes. Brown leather shoes, quite expensive-looking but practical, with thick black rubber soles. Her first thought is Patrick, with a leap of excitement, but of course they can't be his. Had he walked home in socks? Even if he had, could his shoes have lain here for weeks without her seeing them? They can only be Greg's, though that is strange in another way, because it has gone unspoken for months that Greg never visits. Then she understands. It's obvious. He will have come to help Steph move the last of her stuff, and in the middle of helping changed shoes for a more suitable pair, maybe for driving. There are dark patches where rain has soaked into the leather, so evidently there'd been more to do today.

She returns to the living room and finds her phone. Steph answers breathlessly.

Fran!

Hi Steph. Hope you're not in the middle of something?

No, no, no. Just got out the shower.

A tight little laugh between them.

Excellent. I see you've got the last of your stuff now. Well done. I hope it wasn't too arduous?

No, no. I got there.

The house feels so empty. It's the end of an era, Steph.

Aah. I know. But we'll still see each other.

Of course we will. I've been giving the place a clean before the new people look round. You wouldn't recognise it.

Ha! I bet.

I meant to say, I found a pair of Greg's shoes. In case he was looking for them?

Greg's *shoes*?

Yes. They're brown leather. Quite nice.

He does have some brown leather shoes, but he hasn't mentioned losing any.

Could you ask him?

Sure, but he's out at the moment.

Ah. He did help you move, right?

Yes. At the weekend he did. Although it took a few trips and I did most of them on my own. I have more crap than I thought!

Frances watches the fire. Her cheap logs are hissing.

Oh well, she says. I'm sure I'll find a home for them eventually. Could you let me know what he says when you see him? They're nice shoes. Someone will want to know where they are.

Of course.

The other thing was, I don't know what you're up to this evening, but how about one last night in? There's still a huge pile of CDs and DVDs in the front room. I'm sure most of them are yours. We could split a bottle of wine and go through it all, being miserable.

Oh Fran, I'd love to, but I'm actually off to meet Greg at the theatre tonight. I'm just about to get ready.

OK, no problem.

Sorry.

No, that's fine. It was just a thought. We can do it any time.

Well, let's do it soon.

She stares at the fire, then goes back to the shoes. She is struck by the neat way that they sit side by side, insteps touching, laces tucked into the cavities. They look arranged by somebody with opinions on the subject. It is possible she shook water on to them while taking off her coat.

The rain has stopped, but the wind is getting up. Idly she patrols the house, her phone in her hand, not knowing what she's looking for. Between times she goes back to the stock for soothing stirs.

She returns to the sofa and dials her mother, thinking of the phone on its table in the hall. The old phone table. The call connects. She hears her mother's hesitation, then her slightly formal voicemail message, the voice younger than it has become.

Hi Mum. Nothing important really. It's Tuesday evening.

I just phoned to see how you were. Everything's fine here, I don't have any news. I may go out, so don't call back tonight. Talk soon. Bye.

The fire lies low.

She latches and unlatches the laptop with her dialling finger.

She dials my number. It goes to voicemail. She leaves no message.

She goes upstairs and sits on the bed and tucks her legs under herself. She gets up and draws the curtains. She looks at her possessions. The lamp, the wardrobe, the old counterpane on its way back to threads.

She should eat. She remembers the instructions to dice the shallots and garlic finely. Finding the right page, she props the book open with the pepper grinder. The cat smears around her legs. She squeezes out a slab of food and disorders it with a fork. She spoons her own food out too soon. The rice grains have chalky hearts. She is learning. While you learn you eat your mistakes. The washing up done, she revives the fire and watches television with a good apple. She texts Steph to ask what Greg has said about the shoes, but gets no reply. Then she remembers they are at the theatre of course.

She tours the house locking doors and windows and turning off the lights. She washes her hands and from the bathroom cabinet takes two cotton pads, which stick to her wet fingers. The first she presses not quite tight against the mouth of the cleanser bottle, upending them both until a mauve blotch appears. With this she wipes the makeup from her face, then repeats the process with another. Afterwards she applies moisturiser, takes the toothbrush off its base and eases a stump of paste on to the bristles, which she guides for two minutes around her mouth. She flosses while using the toilet.

In the bedroom she undresses and examines herself. When running she imagines her arms like streams of liquid, her hands like splashes. Her hair pulled back makes shining grooves. She still can't find a grey. Steph still has not replied.

Tomorrow she will run her furthest.

She pulls on pyjamas and picks up her book. The sheets grow warm around her. Next door the extractor ceases. Her eyelids start to sag. She flicks ahead and finds a break only a few pages away, but she won't get there. She switches off the light.

Some people say that your mistakes are never really mistakes, which is another way of saying that you intend everything you do, even the unconscious things. I don't feel that way myself, but I suppose I wouldn't. The conscious part of me may be as much in charge as the rider of a horse who proudly steers where he is taken. Or it may not. This isn't something anyone knows. All we know is that we are made of mysteries.

Have you ever wondered how we recognise each other? It feels like a matter of no difficulty at all, but we only know about the feeling. We cannot call to mind exactly what makes a loved one's face their own. That isn't ours to know. It is a mystery. Yet the deeper one in my opinion is how we manage to go through life without considering it mysterious. A hidden power controls our minds and drives our dreams and we hardly think about it. Which movements of your jaw, lips and tongue are required to speak your name? You don't even know. It's almost a miracle of inattentiveness, next to which it seems quite easy to believe that I am only half of who I am, and that you are too. That we blithely share this world with our own ghosts.

I've come to think that this explains the shoes. Taking them off on wet days to avoid leaving footprints on her carpet was a matter of habit. Sometimes I carried them in my bag as I went about my business, but they made everything else in the bag dirty, so I took to leaving them in the hall with a plan to remember, then forgot. Was this carelessness? Things have been easier lately. I won't say easy, but there's been more sleep and routine, and periods of calm, which breeds complacency, as I have warned, so at first that's how I saw things, and berated myself for the blunder. However, after some thought I've come to believe it was the deliberate work of my other half, a wise region of my mind that was unknown to me until eight hours ago, and to which I am blessedly grateful.

She seemed to be acting normally. Without Stephanie these days there's less to overhear, but I clearly made out the sounds of cooking, heard her potter about the house and start the dryer. She was a soothing companion for my writing. When she began to mop the kitchen floor, I took the opportunity to wash. I keep a water container, liquid soap, a plastic bowl and towels. Plus of course I have a makeshift bed in here, a compact camping toilet, my laptop, tools and odds and ends and, these days, most of my clothes. I need something to refresh me during the long hours of stillness and confinement, to reset what at times feels like a very slow clock, and I've found that nothing works better than a wash and a change. I have to manage in low light, but it's a small space. The glow of the laptop screen suffices.

Replacing the headphones, I heard she'd made a fire. I drank coffee from the lid of my flask and listened, quite content and unsuspicious until her call to Stephanie. Instantly I knew what I'd done, but searched for my shoes anyway in a hopeful frenzy. Then my phone was ringing. *Frances B*, it said. *Frances B.* I found my bag and pulled the hammer out, and a roll of tape. I stuffed my pockets with cable ties. I crouched, ready but terrified. I don't think I've ever been so scared. Doing nothing in these situations is I suppose either the worst plan or the best. I waited a long time to find out which.

These were my thinking hours. Now I feel calm. Better than calm. She's had her dinner and is watching television. It seems my shoes have stopped being a mystery she expects to solve by morning, and I've had time to change plans. I'm sad that we won't have our date on Friday. It's been one of those nice stored anticipations, you know, a recurrent little happiness to toy with, but it was always a mistake. I would have been pretending. I'm only glad that I heard my other half in time.

Now she's given up and is locking the doors and turning off the lights. She's washing. She's getting undressed. I sit for a long time in darkness feeling the warmth of the chimney breast beneath my palm. I let her reach deep sleep.

I switch on my torch and change clothes again. I want her to see me dressed as I was the first time, in the checked shirt with the navy pullover and jeans, relaxed but serious. I lift the hatch from the floor and place it to one side across two joists. I tie a length of rope to the handles of my bag and lower it through the hole. Unwinding the thicker rope from its fixings on the rafters, I switch off my torch and grip it in my teeth. I pause, take a deep breath through my nose, and slide down from the loft into the blackness. I feel the landing carpet meet my socks.

YOU SLEEP. THE CURVE OF YOUR CHEEK. The point of your chin. The soft wisps at the margin of your hairline. Your lashes chatter. The duvet rises and falls below your throat. Outside the wind is loud, but get close and your breath can be heard whispering. Get closer still and it can be felt like a feather. Your breath explores the canyons of my ear.

I could leave. There is still time. I could walk downstairs, put on my shoes and dissolve into the wind. Instead I climb on to the bed and switch on your light.

As a young man, even as a boy, I was frustrated, as the young are, by what seemed to me the timidity and the cynicism of older people. I should stress that this was not the arrogance that it was taken for. I inwardly admitted older people's greater knowledge and experience. My argument was that you can have too much. You can gather knowledge and experience in the belief that they will help you solve the problem of what to do with your life, but gradually get nowhere, then quickly say you've discovered that the problem is unsolvable and, therefore, that your failure is success. After a while all the old seemed to know was the comfort of surrender, and for this they were called wise.

Older myself now, I've begun to see things differently, as I feared I would, but not for the reasons I feared. Because the young do not yet know how it feels to be wrong about things. Not just mistaken. Life pounds the young often enough with their mistakes. I mean wrong profoundly, about a religion, about your abilities or shortcomings, about someone you once loved, or didn't. As you age you gather these memories of yourself being wrong in ways that at the time you could not understand. This is how people grow, not just upwards but like trees, by accumulating skins. Each you contains and conceals all the preceding, and none can know the next. After a while you've been so often corrected that you go about in a kind of flinch.

I think humanity is old now. Writing gave us memory, and memory gave us age. The store of what we know goes only upwards. Soon our last beliefs will be blurred away.

Frances.

A bright light and something fussing with your face. Something on your stomach and a hissing sound, a hushing sound. Something hard is on your face, pressing.

Frances.

A man's voice. My voice. I am sitting on you, my knees on either side. My hand is tight on your mouth, burying your head in the pillow. My other hand holds your right wrist. You struggle momentarily and groan but I'm heavy. You stop to reflect.

Listen, Frances. I know you're scared but you're safe. OK? You're safe. I can't let you go because you need to listen to me. Will you listen to me?

At this point you remember the navy wool and my original hair and you nod. You nod and nod. All the fear goes into nodding. I am bright in the light of your lamp.

Thank you. This is frightening. I understand that, but I have something I want to give you and this is the only way.

I smell fragrant. I let go of your wrists but I keep my hand on your mouth. Slowly and smoothly you cross your arms over your chest.

I'm sure you have many questions, but I want you to wait. I'm sorry about this. It's necessary.

You expected something but did not expect something like this.

Do you understand?

You lie still, staring.

Just nod your head if you understand.

You nod your head.

You can sit up if you like, I say. But you need to promise not to speak or scream. I'm going to take my hand away, and I'm going to need to trust you. Can I do that?

You nod.

If you scream, I don't know. I don't really have a plan. That's why this has to work on trust.

You nod again, so I climb off the bed. At first you don't move at all, then you put your palms on the mattress and raise yourself, revealing blue pyjamas. You shuffle back against the headboard, smuggling in a glance around the room. Your phone is missing, and your clock has been turned to face the wall. A cup of tea steams next to it. I have my own on the floor, and a bag.

I'm sorry, Frances.

You see fear in my eyes too.

I sit beside you on the bed with the bag on my lap and sip my tea. You look at the bag.

That's for you, I say with a gesture at your cup.

You aren't sure. You stare.

It's OK. It's just a cup of tea.

You lift it to your mouth and take some sips. I get mine and do the same. Our eyes meet over the brims, your eyes and mine. It's like there's something that you're meant to understand. You think about dousing me with tea. You don't know if it's still hot enough to burn, or if you need me to be burned. You need to escape. You'd fling off the covers and run. Then I'd be after you, and you might be caught, and the struggle might become something. Besides, I must have thought of this. I've surely locked the doors or brought a weapon or something, if I have any sense. Do I have any sense? You look at me. I look so kind. I look almost normal. I was kind and normal in the cafe. Rare ways of being, though they seem so little to ask. You want to believe that I'm about to give you an innocent explanation for what I'm doing, and I look like I am, but then it scares you that invading your bedroom at night seems so innocent to me. That I can sit by your legs and drink tea. Am I pretending to be normal, or pretending to be scary? Maybe I don't make those decisions any more. Maybe that's what it means to be mad. Maybe this is just going to be a weird night that you'll always remember, and in the morning I'll go back with the orderlies. Maybe burning me with tea, smashing the window, screaming, maybe they would change the kind of night that this will be. You can't presume to know what the mad intend. Right now you're unharmed, you're free to move. Maybe these things happen all the time and are seldom reported. Maybe it's only selection bias that's making you think there's rape and murder in my bag. You try to stop looking at it. You don't want to remind me.

You remember a story you heard not long ago from a friend, the story of a young woman who woke in her hotel room to find a man standing over her. He made flustered claims, then fled. She called reception who promised to send someone instantly, but when someone arrived it was the same man in different clothes. She'd been sleepy the first time, there'd been less light, but she knew him despite his denials. She found another hotel and the story petered out, but she still wonders what he wanted. He probably just wanted her underwear. Or maybe underwear's how they start. You could offer me some underwear. I might be offended, and you were warned not to talk. You wonder if the man in the hotel had a bag.

You drink tea and try a smile to appease me.

I am sorry, I say. We can still have that drink on Friday. I did want to wait until then, but I've thought about it since, and we have to do this first.

I raise a hand. You were about to speak.

Please, I say. You'll get an explanation. First let's just enjoy our tea.

My calm has gone. I need this pause to recover. Patrick was easy, I now realise. I didn't care what he thought. I feel bad about that sometimes, how little he meant to me, how much I resented the mess he left behind. You might say I feel bad because I don't feel worse. I'd listen to anything you say. This is why I don't want you to speak. And of course you don't know me yet. That was once the way I wanted it. Now I want us together, which means the old human difficulty again, the yearning for love and the whether or not we get it. Ask most people, ask society, and they say the way to be loved is to act loveable, which if you ask me is as dumb as it gets. I've seen them time and again, these loveable fictions. I don't want somebody to love my act.

You finish your tea and I finish mine. I place my hands in my lap, imitating your body language, you notice, which you consider a good sign.

I sit silently until I realise that you're waiting for me. I had quite a tight script, and you're doing your part beautifully, but I'm constantly forgetting my lines and having to improvise.

Look, I say, unzipping the bag. You've waited a long time, and I want you to know what that means to me. You could have got bored in the cafe, or decided I wasn't coming. I don't know. Most people just wouldn't keep it up. They'd worry about being thought strange. You didn't worry. Or maybe you did, but you carried on. Whatever happens, I want you to know now that that means everything. That can't be faked.

You did worry. You worried a lot at first, but the fear of being unoccupied was stronger. Then waiting was a habit.

By the end I was like a myth to you, and a prophecy. The return of the writer who was kind. You didn't want to tell Dawn but you'd begun to wonder if I was real. If maybe you'd imagined me to meet an emotional need at a stressful time. No one else you know has met me, besides Patrick, who has since become a ghost himself. Now you wonder what I've been doing all the while.

So look, I say.

You watch me going through my things. You see a length of rope. Is that the shaft of a hammer? You pray. You never pray. At last I produce a tablet computer.

I want you to read this.

You look confused.

I wrote it for you, I say. It's not finished and I don't know how to end it, but it's something I've been working on for a while.

You see that I look desperate, but I want you to focus on the book, not on me. I am not who I am.

If you want to understand what's going on, this book will help. I want you to read it.

You are scared but you are curious. *Consent*, says the title page. You flick through the others and see something about a *Laura*. You see your own name, and the email mentioned. It appears to be an account of my behaviour.

Just start from the beginning. It's not perfect, but I've tried to be honest. I've told you everything I can. Read it through and then we'll talk.

You raise your knees to make a desk for the book, then hesitate.

It's short. I might write more, but just read what there is

for now. Maybe you could help me finish it? As you'll see I'm in a muddle about how it ends.

You wonder if you could email the authorities, but you can't see an internet connection and you don't dare alert me with your finger strokes. I wait by the door, watching. I look on edge.

Are you cold?

You shrug, so I get your dressing gown from the back of the door and help you into it.

Tired? I have some modafinil. It will help.

You shake your head and look back at the page, meaning to start, but it isn't easy. Your mind is vigilant and won't submit. Whole paragraphs slip by with not a word absorbed. You draw little spirals with your index finger on your cheek. You probably don't realise.

I step forwards and reach into my bag. You are ready to spring for the door, but I only pull out my copy of Montaigne. I hope to put you at your ease by appearing lost in it. When I look over, your eyes are wide and dark, with a bright pip of the screen.

—

I know you're reading this and I want to talk to you, but I don't know what to say.

You're scared. I know. I get scared as well. It's OK but it's a distraction. Maybe if you're scared constantly you stop noticing? Maybe always being afraid is the path to calm times.

Whenever I hear about someone dying I always think

how strange it is that we are here to talk about it, that our world continues while theirs has been annihilated. Can that be right? Even with practice I don't think I've got any better at believing it, let alone believing it will happen to me. I suppose death lives further from us these days.

People often talk about the wondrous size of the universe, about the billions of stars in the billions of galaxies and the billions of years that they've been around. They say that it makes their life feel meaningless, and maybe it does, but that isn't the effect on me. When I contemplate all the other worlds out there it threatens to be more meaningful than I can cope with. This is what it's like to be me. Like this, and lonely. Being alone, how else should I feel?

How about being you? What is that like? I want to know, and I've tried to imagine. I've really thought about the details, but I fear I've made mistakes. Tell me the truth. Did I get it right?